T0268403

CONVOY TO MOROCCO

Convoy to Morocco

A Riley Fitzhugh Novel

Terry Mort

Essex, Connecticut

McBooks
Press

An imprint of Globe Pequot, the trade division of
The Rowman & Littlefield Publishing Group, Inc.
4501 Forbes Blvd., Ste. 200
Lanham, MD 20706
www.rowman.com

Distributed by NATIONAL BOOK NETWORK

British Library Cataloguing in Publication Information available

Library of Congress Cataloging-in-Publication Data available
ISBN 978-1-4930-5840-2 (hardback: alk. paper)
ISBN 978-1-4930-7150-0 (e-book)

∞™ The paper used in this publication meets the minimum requirements of American National
Standard for Information Sciences—Permanence of Paper for Printed Library Materials, ANSI/
NISO Z39.48-1992.

Author's Note

The adventures of Riley Fitzgerald and the *Nameless* are fiction, but the stories of the merchant ship, *Contessa*, and the French Sebou River pilot, Rene Malevergne, are factual. Malevergne was awarded the Navy Cross for his service. Also factual are the overall context and strategy of Operation TORCH, as well as events depicted in the battle, including the role of the USS *Dallas*.

Chapter One

"Have you ever wanted to sail the seas on a tramp steamer?"

"No."

He looked at me in mock disbelief.

"No? Never dreamed of a voyage through the steaming tropics? Exotic ports of call? Lusty, dark-eyed women in sarongs? Degenerate planters sweating in white linen suits? Gone-to-seed half-castes? Sinister Lascar crewmen? Something out of *Lord Jim*?"

"No. And if I remember correctly, things didn't turn out so well for Lord Jim."

"Well, no. But life does not have to imitate art."

"Good to know."

"Well, I must say, I'm surprised."

"That'll be the day." As far as I could tell, Bunny had never been surprised about anything in his forty-some years. If he ever had been, he certainly wouldn't have shown it.

We were sitting in the library of his club, Bellamy's, on St James's Street. Bunny was a British intelligence officer assigned as a liaison to the Americans' OSS. His real name was Dennis Finch-Hayden, but he was nicknamed Bunny by an evil nanny, and it stuck. He liked the name, because he had a refined taste for irony. He was decidedly un-bunny-like—tall, angular, beaky, and elegant. Women thought he was devastatingly good-looking and charming. He reminded me of Ichabod Crane. I had known him back in Los Angeles when I was a PI and he was a professor of art at UCLA. We had worked on a couple of forgery cases together. Most recently, as in just the few last weeks, we had worked on a clandestine mission in Morocco. Or rather, I was in Morocco, while

Bunny managed from London. So not exactly "together." I'd been sent to gather intelligence that would be useful to the planners of Operation Torch, the upcoming Anglo-American invasion of North Africa. "Upcoming" as in next month.

"I was sure the idea of a tramp steamer would appeal to someone with your romantic nature," he said.

"My romantic nature begins and ends with blondes."

That wasn't really true. I exclude no one on the basis of hair color. But it was a good B movie line.

"Really? What about Amanda Billingsgate?"

"She was platinum the last time I saw her."

"Ah. She always was a chameleon, our Amanda."

"That's one word for her." Amanda was our "mutual friend," as Dickens put it. There are pedants around who complain that it's an incorrect use of the word "mutual," but most people understand what Dickens meant.

"Where is she, by the way?" I said.

"Amanda? Ah, who can say? She's like the Scarlet Pimpernel—'they seek her here, they seek her there, they seek her everywhere.'"

There were only a few things I really knew about Amanda. I knew she was a spy, but I wasn't sure who for. Could be both sides. I also knew she was either a very good, or a very lucky, hand with a pistol. She had shot at least two men that I knew of—potted both of them just below their widow's peak. One was her husband. She said it was an accident. There were people who believed her. I also knew she wasn't a platinum blond. More of a butterscotch. And I knew you couldn't trust her. But I didn't care so much about that. Most of the time it didn't matter. You knew everything about her was temporary. Well, tell me something that isn't. Just enjoy the butterscotch while it lasts.

Amanda was along for the ride in Morocco when I was there. That was when she shot the second of her male victims. I saw her do it. It was an accident that way the Germans going into Poland was an accident.

"I suppose there's a reason for your question about the tramp steamer," I said. Bunny had a reason for everything.

"Well, yes. Something has come up, and when I heard of it, I thought of you immediately."

"No, thanks. I'm expecting orders to return to my ship. They're just about finished putting her back together."

"Yes, I know. But you might change your mind after you've heard the offer I have for you," he said. "It's the chance you've never longed for."

"Uh huh."

I knew what all this meant. It meant I was still in the grip of the intelligence boys. I had been expecting to be released from my temporary OSS assignment and sent back to my ship, which was in Scotland undergoing extensive repairs from our last frightful convoy duty, when part of the superstructure was blown off by a bomb from a Heinkel 111. But apparently the Navy, and through them, the OSS, had other plans for me. And as for this "offer," there was really no such thing in the service. There were "orders" and there were "volunteer missions," and there was almost no difference between the two. One was like shooting a sitting duck, while the other was like yelling "SHOO!" a split second before pulling the trigger. There was a slight technical difference, maybe, but in either case the result was the same loss of feathers. And the odds were very good that Bunny had my "volunteer" orders in the inside breast pocket of his Savile Row suit, next to his blue and white Eton tie. He'd make his sales pitch, I'd agree, and he'd give me the orders. That was how it was supposed to work.

"Well, it's an interesting situation," he said. "You'll be intrigued, I'm sure. Care for a drink before we get down to the exciting details? Or should I say opportunities?"

"Make it a double."

Bunny called down to the bar and in a few moments, Job, the ancient waiter, came creeping into the library with a tray of drinks. Over in nearby Green Park a bomb went off and rattled the club's windows, but neither Bunny nor Job seemed to notice—Job, because he was a little deaf, and Bunny because he was Bunny. The worst days of the Blitz were over, but now and then the Germans would send over reminders. I never could tell whether Bunny's sangfroid was genuine or assumed. I asked him one time about that, and he merely quoted something about appearance being reality and after all, what did it matter? There were lots of things about Bunny that were never quite clear.

"How's life treating you, Job?" he asked, pleasantly.

"Couldn't be better, sir, thank you."

"Good for you. How's the wife?"

"I often wonder, sir."

Job put down the tray and crept away.

"Job is our resident optimist. He and his wife have an understanding, based on mutual dislike. Very civilized." Was this the proper use of "mutual," I wondered? I thought so. "Well, cheerio."

"Right," I said, sourly.

"Relax, my friend. I promise that you will enjoy this next assignment, assuming you decide to volunteer for it. Of course, I have no doubts that you will, when you hear what I have to say."

"Neither do I, somehow."

Chapter Two

It involved Operation Torch, and a return to Casablanca.

Torch would be a three-pronged Anglo-American invasion of two French colonies in North Africa—Morocco and Algeria. The Brits would swoop down through the Straits of Gibraltar and hit two spots in Algeria. Morocco, and specifically the port city, Casablanca, would be an all-American show, involving a massively intricate and difficult transatlantic amphibious attack. Once captured, Casablanca would become a key supply port for subsequent Allied operations in North Africa, where the Germans were already running rampant in Libya and Egypt and needed to be evicted. North Africa, once secured, would then become a jumping-off point for an invasion of Europe, through what Churchill called its "soft underbelly." Well, just how soft it was remained to be seen. But first things first.

The great unknown in all of this was whether the French military and colonial government, who were nominally loyal to the Vichy government, would put up any resistance. Maybe they'd welcome us as liberators. But maybe they wouldn't. We did know that some of the French troops and their officers, in particular, gave more than lip service loyalty to Vichy. In fact, they were staunchly devoted to the French government that had surrendered to the Germans. The Vichy leader was old Marshall Petain, a hero of the First War and a man whose word was law to most of the professional French military. The Germans were now occupying half of France and letting Petain's collaborationists run the southern half from the new capital at Vichy. Just how long that tricky relationship would last was anybody's guess, but everyone knew it depended on Vichy toeing the line, not only in France, but also in their colonies, especially Morocco and Algeria. The French still had nominal control of the African colonies, but German Armistice Commissions, along with Gestapo agents, infested the colonies to keep an eye on their new French partners. The French naval officers in Africa were especially loyal to Vichy. They were still seething over the earlier British attack on the Algerian naval base at Mers El Kebir. That attack crippled the French fleet and killed thirteen hundred French sailors. After pleading with the French navy to sail away to the Americas and sit out the war, or at the very least scuttle their ships, Churchill had ordered the attack, because he was afraid the French ships would fall into German hands and render the British position in the Mediterranean untenable. The lifeline to Suez would be cut. It was a cold-blooded decision that understandably still rankled and made it impossible to know just how the French professional brass would react when we showed up in force. There was also good reason to believe that some French professional officers were not all that upset about the German takeover. True, they were embarrassed about the utter debacle and the humiliation of defeat, but they were now claiming it was largely the result of the softness of politicians and rottenness at the core of French political culture. As for the French navy, well, they could tell themselves that they weren't the ones who lost. They hadn't really been in it. Furthermore, they viewed the attack on Mers El Kebir as typical of "perfidious Albion." They haven't liked the British for the last few centuries, anyway, and that attack just confirmed their ancestral view that the British were not only a nation of shopkeepers, but a bunch of treacherous bastards, to boot. In short, there was plenty of reason to wonder how the French would greet us when we splashed ashore in their North African colonies. They liked us Yanks a little, certainly more than they liked the Brits, which was not at all. But we couldn't expect to win their hearts and minds with Hershey Bars and Lucky Strikes. They might not like to shoot at us Yanks, but their sense of embarrassed national honor might require it. Did Burr really intend to kill Hamilton? Hard to say, but when it was over, Hamilton was just as dead.

One key to our Casablanca invasion plan was the Sebou River. The Sebou debouches into the Atlantic about fifty miles north of the coastal port city of Casablanca. The river is an oxbow shape and on the map the eastern half looks like Kilroy's nose hanging over a fence. At the end of its twelve-mile navigable stretch sits the town of Port Lyautey and a French army base. The army's there to protect the only concrete airstrip in North Africa. That means that it's the only airfield that can accommodate heavy bombers. Part of the plan of attack on Casablanca involved capturing the airport at Port Lyautey, not only to neutralize potential French air force resistance, but also to provide a base for Allied fighter aircraft that would be brought in via a converted aircraft transport. Unlike an attack carrier, the transport could launch planes but not recover them, and so the airport would be needed as a landing spot and future base. Once ashore, the planes would need refueling and rearming, which meant a supply ship would somehow have to navigate the tricky waters of the Sebou to deliver supplies to refuel the planes that would be coming in. In addition to being shallow, the river was tidal and subject to shifting sands and shoals. Our Navy transports drew too much water to make the trip. Most merchant vessels of requisite capacity did, too.

So the Sebou River was an important piece of the invasion puzzle. As a result, I had been sent there to extract a river pilot with knowledge of the river's idiosyncrasies. One way or another, when the time came, he would "volunteer" to pilot a merchant ship loaded with supplies and assault troops up the river to the airport. Unbeknownst to me, though, the Machiavellian planners in the OSS, to which my friend Bunny was assigned as liaison, used me as a decoy, while they spirited a real river pilot, a man named Rene Malevergne, out of Morocco. The Frenchman I was simultaneously shepherding out of Morocco was also a river pilot, but his specialty was not the Sebou River. In fact, he had come to North Africa only recently, where he had fallen on hard times and resorted to petty crime. He didn't know the Sebou from the Seine. With the help of one treacherous platinum blonde, he "eluded" me in Tangier and was allowed to fall into the hands of the Germans, who would ask him politely why we had such an interest in him, and he, knowing no more about any of this than I did, would give them a Gallic shrug and reveal his history as a pilot on the Rhône River. He was utterly believable and could not be shaken, because he was simply telling the truth. The object was to let the Germans—and their Vichy stooges—deduce that we were

7

planning an invasion up the Rhône River into the south of France, so that when we actually arrived in North Africa in force, *Quelle bloody surprise!* It was, I had to admit, a very neat plan, even though I was a decoy leading another decoy, and like all decoys we had no notion of what we were really doing or why.

"Your chaps call it 'disinformation,' old boy," said Bunny, after I got back and learned what really happened. "Not a very elegant term. I prefer 'subterfuge.' But if it works, so much the better, whatever you call it. You know what Shakespeare said about roses. And I have no doubt you'll get a medal for your derring-do."

So I was being praised for doing something I did not know I was doing, while thinking all the while I was doing something else. If P.G. Wodehouse had written this script, I would have played the role of Bertie Wooster and the OSS, especially Bunny, would have been a collective Jeeves. Well, as Bertie would say, "Right-Ho." It all worked out in the end. At least I didn't get shot for my troubles, though there were some moments when it looked like I might.

"After all," said Bunny, "how many heroes know what they're doing at the time they're doing it?"

"I doubt many were as completely clueless as I was."

"I doubt it, too," he said with a smile. "But you also got to spend some quality time with Amanda Billingsgate. Surely that compensates for any chagrin you might feel about being mildly duped."

As a matter of fact, it did. Somewhat.

"What was it Mark Antony said about Cleopatra?" said Bunny. "'Other women cloy the appetite they feed; she makes hungry where she most satisfies.' Something like that. Amanda to a T, no?"

"Yes. Something like that. I suppose you speak from experience." That wouldn't surprise me, because Amanda liked a bit of variety, when choosing her love affairs.

"Oh, I couldn't possibly comment," said Bunny. "But whatever might have happened was in the dimmest past, and we're really just pals. Or were before she went over to the Germans. Happily she took your Rhône River pilot with her, just as we hoped she would."

"After slipping me what the Hollywood gangsters call a mickey."

"Yes. Has the wound healed?"

"More or less. Since you brought that up, are we sure she really did? Go over to the Germans? It occurred to me that you clever boys in the spy business might have inserted her as a double agent."

"Did it? Well, who can say? But are we ever sure of anything? You know what the philosopher Hume said about that kind of thing."

"Not offhand."

"I forget. Something very brainy, I'm sure. But we were talking about the Sebou River. The good news is that Rene Malevergne has graciously volunteered to pilot a cargo ship up the lazy river, to quote Hoagy Carmichael. And we've only just been able to locate a useful ship for him to drive. Rene, that is. It wasn't that easy to find a merchant ship that had the right characteristics and was also available for the job."

What was needed was a merchant steamer that had sufficient cargo capacity and yet had a shallow enough draft to make it up the river.

"You can't seriously be telling me that the whole Casablanca plan depends on getting some merchant tub up a shallow river, so that we can fight our way onto an airfield to get air cover. Surely not."

"No. Your people are going to send a proper attack carrier as part of the invasion fleet, so there should be plenty of combat air cover. This is just one piece of the puzzle, but we'd like it if it came off as planned. We absolutely do need to secure the airfield, undamaged if possible, both for this mission and beyond. If we can't get a supply ship upriver, we'll have to send troops and supply vehicles over land to get to the airfield. And there are some tricky marshes between the coast and the airfield. And some French troops in positions that will have to be taken. So the whole plan doesn't rest on this particular mission. However—this *is* Plan A. It's by far the best option. So it would be very good, if it comes off. Very good, indeed."

"This is my cue for asking where I fit in—assuming I volunteer, of course."

"Yes. Of course. It involves the ship itself. She's the SS *Carlota*, and she's owned by the United Fruit Company—a genuine banana boat. She has spent the last decade or so going back and forth between South American river plantations and the US. Hence the shallow draft. Some of those riverside plantations are pretty far inland and deep in the jungle. The rivers are tricky, much like the Sebou. Now and then *Carlota* would take passengers as well as fruit, so she's not bereft of creature comforts. But she is an elderly civilian vessel manned by civilian crew—the usual ragbag of nationalities. Or at least she was. When we acquired her for this mission, most of the crew scattered and headed for the hills. No way of making them stay, obviously. A few did, but not enough. The ones who did are not the kind you'd want to take home to mother, I'm afraid. And your Navy personnel boys weren't at all helpful in finding replacements, because they are stretched to the limit of resources for the Torch invasion fleet. There aren't enough sailors to man the navy ships, let alone the *Carlota*. So, after a bit of wrangling and arm twisting, we were able to find some men—merchant seamen, who were available and willing to sign on."

"Do I dare ask where you got them?"

"In the Norfolk, Virginia, jail."

"I see. Jaywalkers? Ticket scofflaws?"

"Yes, something along those lines. Anyway, the good news is there's enough of them to get underway and make the trip. The officers of the ship have volunteered, bless 'em, and the skipper is an old hand—an Aussie named Flynn. First name, Elmer."

"Not Errol."

"No. But don't let that worry you. He is quite used to dicey situations. There were several incidents involving the usual revolutionaries in South American trying to capture the *Carlota* during one of her upriver jaunts to plantations. A shootout or two. But Flynn acquitted himself admirably. He potted at least one rebel. Knocked him off his burro with a Webley .45 at twenty-five yards. A very decent shot. Usually those things aren't accurate much beyond ten feet. So you need have no qualms about his fitness."

"And what am I to do about all this? What's the job?"

"Well, this is a mission that requires a naval guard. What's more, the *Carlota* is being fitted with a three-inch fifty gun. Manual aiming, of course. No time or money to install radar fire control."

"Useless against aircraft."

"Yes. I'm afraid so. But handy in case a U-boat surfaces and decides to use her deck gun, instead an expensive torpedo. The *Carlota*'s gun will need an experienced Navy crew to man it. And it will need an officer in command. It's the kind of thing you're familiar with."

"I suppose so. But any gunnery officer could handle this job. Why me?"

"Ah. That is the question, to quote the Bard. We're pretty sure about Rene and Flynn, the skipper, and the exec seems OK. A Brit. Down-at-the-heels, but apparently reliable. But we're less sure about a few of the crew. Not that they're foreign agents, but just that they might not be willing to play by the rules, once they're released."

"Or once they have a better idea of what they've signed on for."

"Yes. So we'd like one of our own on scene to make sure that everyone is playing the game."

"That could be done by any junior officer."

"Yes. Well, it might surprise you to know that inter-service politics enters just a bit into this assignment."

"What's that French expression again?"

"*Quelle surprise*? Yes, I suppose so. So far the whole Sebou River and *Carlota* plan has been an OSS show. And we're the new boys in the cloak and dagger business—regarded with more than a little suspicion by the other intelligence agencies. Which means it's important for inter-service politics that our part of this comes off reasonably well."

"What you really mean is it's important for OSS credibility and future."

"If you like. The idea of plucking a Sebou River pilot was ours, and we've done it, thanks in part to you. We want to finish the job."

"And also to secure the credit the OSS feels it would deserve."

"Well, yes. As usual there are wheels within wheels and issues of funding future ideas and operations. And success in this venture would be very valuable to the team. I know it sounds childish, but politics are childish, by definition. A fact of life, unfortunately. And since at the moment you are just waiting around for your own ship to be repaired, we thought you might like to take on this assignment. After all, you have nothing else to do . . . and . . ." He paused and looked at me slyly, "You are still more or less part of *our* team."

"Meaning there are no new orders for me to report back to my ship."

"Not quite yet. But I think I can promise you that, by the time you make the crossing, your own ship will be ready and waiting to join in the Torch invasion. You can rejoin her off the coast of Casablanca."

"Do I really have a choice?"

"Of course you do. I'm reminded of a scene in Mark Twain when an old west stagecoach traveler stops at a frontier outpost and asks for dinner, and the manager says 'We have stewed coyote and mustard,' and the traveler says 'But I don't like stewed coyote,' and the manager says 'Well, then, help yourself to the mustard.'"

"I see."

"That might not be the exact quote, but you get the gist."

"Yes. As a matter of interest, what's the *Carlota*'s cargo?"

"Just what you'd expect. Bombs and aviation petrol. Gas, I should say."

"Ah!"

"Best not to run into a torpedo."

"Words to live by. When will that be loaded? Not before the crossing, I hope. In England, maybe? Or from an underway replenishment?"

"I think it's being loaded as we speak. In Norfolk. Virginia, not England. That's the plan, anyway."

"So we'll be hauling the stuff across the Atlantic. And you consider that story good salesmanship?" A ship loaded with that kind of cargo wouldn't have time to sink when torpedoed. It would just disappear in a very large fireball followed by a dense cloud of smoke. "Missing, presumed dead" would be our epitaph. No need to worry about where to send the bodies; there wouldn't be any. "No wonder the crew all scattered."

"Not all of them. And besides, you'll be in a convoy. A part of the whole fleet. Not much danger in that."

"Out of curiosity, how big is the fleet?"

"A hundred, warships and transports. This is a gigantic operation. The biggest ever tried."

"Complex."

"You have no idea. But you will, assuming you volunteer, of course."

"Of course."

"The Casablanca part of Torch alone means getting over a hundred ships across the Atlantic and arriving at the same spot at the same time and putting 35,000 troops ashore, in Atlantic surf and possibly under fire. Such a thing has never been done. Most of your top brass wanted nothing to do with it. The order came from Roosevelt, himself. More politics. The Allies had to be seen to be doing something."

"The Second Front Stalin's been clamoring for."

"Yes. Our people are afraid Uncle Joe might throw in the towel and make a separate peace. Lord knows he's capable of anything. There's no doubt Uncle Joe's a dangerous madman. But he's our dangerous madman—at least until we get rid of the one in Berlin."

"Strange bedfellows we have."

"Well, you know what the philosopher Hume said about that."

"Not offhand."

"Something or other. It'll come to me. Anyway, the planning for Torch has been frantic, because it has to happen as soon as possible and certainly before winter weather makes the whole thing impossible. But you know the old adage—a plan usually only works until first contact with the enemy, then it all becomes a matter of adjustment and improvisation."

"Or panic and chaos."

"Possibly. Let's hope our improvisation is like your New Orleans jazz—creative, but within a melody you can more or less recognize." He paused for a moment and grinned. "Well, what do you say to our little proposition?"

"Just what you expect me to say."

"Ah, good! Help yourself to the mustard."

CHAPTER THREE

I HAD READ THAT MUSTARD ANECDOTE IN *ROUGHING IT* AND REMEM-
bered that the actual dish being offered was mackerel, not stewed coyote.
But I thought Bunny's version was actually better. It's not often anyone
can improve on Mark Twain, but in this case I think Bunny did, so I
didn't say anything. Besides, even Twain said the story was an old and
hoary one, so if he borrowed it, there was no reason not to borrow it
again. And there was something of more immediate concern.

"You said I'd be in charge of a naval guard—regular Navy men. But
you also said the whole Torch operation is shorthanded."

"Yes, I'm afraid so. But I feel certain you'll be able to deal with things
when you get to Norfolk."

"Well, suppose I wanted some of my men from the 475?" The 475
was the hull number of my patrol craft, nicknamed the "Nameless" by
the crew, because she had no proper name. None of the PCs did. Just
numbers.

"Not a bad thought."

"I have a unit that has a little training in small arms, and we have
actually been in a firefight and some interesting shore action against the
enemy."

"Yes. I read about that action in Cuba. That was well done."

"Thank you. But I think our men would be much better than a collection of random sailors, and they're just sitting around waiting while the
civilian yardbirds do the work on *Nameless*. I know these guys, like them
and can trust them. They call themselves Fitzy's Fubars."

"Meaning?"

"It's a Yank acronym. What do you say? Could you make it happen? Throw the switch on your deus ex machina?"

"Give me a list of their names."

And that's how the Fubars temporarily joined the OSS.

I took the next available C54 transport heading for Prestwick, Scotland. From there it would be another transport to the States with overnight stops in Iceland and Labrador. I had thought about going to the Clyde River shipyards before I left and meeting with the Fubars and the skipper, one Tom aka "Model T" Ford. But the orders for the men hadn't been cut yet, and frankly I didn't really want to face the skipper. He wouldn't be all that happy about my kidnapping six of his men, even with a firm OSS promise to return them once the *Nameless* got underway—presumably to join the Torch invasion. The men would have orders to show up in Norfolk, and I would meet them there and give them the glad tidings that we were going to take a floating bomb across the Atlantic with a crew of jailbirds. For now they could enjoy the mystery of being sent home, if only for a week or so.

Of course I had second thoughts about all of this. That's only natural. But I did agree with Bunny's comment that a ship in a massive convoy like Operation Torch would be pretty safe, regardless of her cargo. The transports would be screened by destroyers and other anti-submarine vessels, and the air would be covered by planes from the attack carrier. So it should be a well-protected passage. The success of the operation depended on it. I wouldn't want to make it alone. But I wouldn't have to. And there was just the sneaking suspicion that doing another favor of sorts for the OSS could turn out to be a good thing. I didn't know how, but I felt sure it would be a useful marker to have in my pocket—if not immediately, then at some point. There would be life after the war, assuming we all made it through, and I had learned that the people in the OSS hierarchy were movers and shakers from all sorts of walks of life. They would be good to know.

Just before I left for Prestwick, Bunny called and said there was some mail for me at the US Embassy.

"One seems to be from your friend in Hollywood," he said. "The other has no return address but smells very good. Dana's Tabu, if I had to guess, although I'm not an expert in such things." No. Of course he wasn't.

I opened the letters on the flight to Prestwick. They were both on those flimsy onion skin sheets that people used for airmail. Hers was dated three weeks ago.

Darling,

Where are you? Can you say? I'm still in Cuba, for my sins, and trying to be thankful for the beautiful weather and not succeeding. I've been sending frantic letters and telegrams to Collier's to try to get another assignment. I'm thinking of flying up to New York the end of this month. If I sit on the right editor's lap, I may be able to arrange something. I can't stay here in tropical paradise much longer without going bats. I know it's not likely that you'll be anywhere close by, but I thought I would mention it in case . . . Well, you know. I'll be staying at the Waldorf. It would be lovely to see you. I'm feeling a little . . . complicated. Sort of Keats-ian, and I know you understand what I mean. I suppose it's because it's autumn—a time "to fill all fruit with ripeness to the core." It's warm down here, this autumn. So I'm sort of dreaming about "Autumn in New York"—do you know that song? "Lovers that bless the dark, on benches in Central Park, greet autumn in New York, it's good to live it again." Mmm.

Write to me when you can.

Love, M

Was there more than one meaning when she said "it's warm down here"? Most likely. She loved double and triple entendres. But if her perfume was called Tabu, it was a joke she was making to herself, more than a provocative signal to me. She certainly wouldn't expect me to identify the scent. She knew I wouldn't know Tabu from Bay Rum. So it was more a sly, secret smile. Somerset Maugham once said the purist type of writer was the one who sits alone and laughs at his own jokes. Martha could do that with the best of them. She also knew that neither one of us really gave much thought to conventional taboos. She lived her life on multiple levels simultaneously, primarily the literal and the ironic. Her romantic imagination was well hidden, though, even from herself, now and then. But that, too, when aroused, was surprisingly intense. And I was the happy beneficiary. She used to say that she and I lived in a parallel reality. We didn't, of course, and we both knew it. But the idea appealed to her when she was feeling poetic. She also had a well-developed sense of indignation, especially over the politics she reported on. She didn't suffer fools at all, and that indignation could make her hard to live with now and then. But I didn't have to live with her. That was her husband's problem. Her complexity was a large part of her charm, I thought—that and the fact that she could be elegant and beautiful when she wanted to be. I thought the French word *ravissante* described her best, especially when she was lying in bed with her eyes half closed from pleasure and her blond hair tousled on the pillow. But she also looked pretty good in her foreign correspondent outfit, too—khaki shirt and pants and combat boots—although most would not call her beautiful, then. But they didn't know her the way I did. I sometimes thought it was a shame she was married. But in another sense, I knew it was much better that way. Did I feel guilty about our affair? Now and then, maybe, but not much. I had met, and even kind of liked, her husband. Kind of. But if I felt a little guilty, I could live with it. Nothing's perfect. Voltaire said, "The best is the enemy of the good." And he got around some, if I'm not mistaken. Besides, it would never dawn on her husband that she was having any sort of romantic affair. It simply wouldn't occur to him, and not just because the two of them were at the end of their trail together. So, as the old Spanish motto had it—"What the eyes to do not see, the heart does not feel." More words to live by. Bunny says that makes me a romantic empiricist. Well, I could live with that, too. Whatever it was.

The other letter was from my friend Hobey Baker, once a famous writer of Jazz Age stories, but now a slightly gone-to-seed Hollywood script writer.

Dear Hornblower,

Ahoy and Shiver Me Timbers! How are you, Old Sport? Still afloat? I sincerely hope so. Things here in Never Never Land are pretty much the same, although I have struck a reasonably mighty blow for the local serfs (also known as writers). You know I have been writing those ten-minute travelogues they show between double features, and for a brief instant I was the fair-haired boy of the genre, because I suggested putting new narration and sound track behind footage from old movies, which would otherwise molder in the archives, like Theda Bara. Much cheaper than sending expensive camera crews around the world shooting natives and scenery. After all, a pig in a puddle could be anywhere, and an Indian is an Indian pretty much everywhere, and even if you need fill out a film with some new stuff, there are always lots of extras sitting around Hollywood doing nothing but complaining about their agents. Easy enough to film them cavorting in Laurel Canyon and say they're in Patagonia or Greenland or wherever. So I pitched an idea for a new ten-minute epic called The Beaches of Bolivia, and it was approved and we produced it using only some old footage from a South Sea Islands movie starring Sabu or someone like that. Brown-ish fellow in a turban. Very impressive surf. But when we screened it for the powers-that-be, some snotty nephew of a big boss said that Bolivia was landlocked. Well, for a minute I was ill at ease. After all, who knew? But suddenly I remembered hearing about a lake down there somewhere called something like Tittykaka, and when I said this was of course what I had in mind, because it was well known for its beaches, the nephew shut up and went back to kissing Uncle's ass. No one seemed to worry that pictures of crashing surf might seem a little out of place in a lake, so the meeting ended with smiles all around. Score one for the proles. "Writers of the world, unite! You have nothing to lose but your Jaguars!" I've also been working on two jobs that have an eerie geographical similarity. The first was a Crosby and Hope Road epic—Road to Morocco. There is a talking camel in it, and I rewrote a couple of lines for it. Sheer poetry. It was a two humper and I don't know whether that's a dromedary or a camel. The camel on a pack of cigarettes is a one humper, and the critter in the movie had two, so I guess they're from two different species, like men

*and women. But I don't suppose it matters. I don't expect too much in
the way of screen credit for this work, but I did get a check and free
lunch at the commissary, so score one for the good guys. I've also been
doing some script doctoring on the latest Bogart movie, tentatively
called Casablanca. (You see the Morocco connection. These things run
in twos.) It's scheduled for release around the end of the year. Ingrid
Bergman is the female lead, and one look at her eyes welling up with
tears is enough to make you want to run away from home. They're
thinking that the last shot of the movie will show Bogie and his pal
played by Claude Rains walking off into a fog bank, and the studio
boys said the ending needed a punchy line. Something memorable. I
submitted, "I wonder if there are any white women in Brazzaville."
I don't know whether they'll use it. Speaking of humps, Hedda sends
you her regards and affection. Or she would if she thought about it.
She's in a little hot water, because one of the pathetic people who wrote
to her for advice actually took it and committed suicide, even though
any sane person would know that Hedda was being ironic when she
suggested it. Some people are so literal minded. But this too shall pass.
Her column's too popular to can. The whole gang of degenerates here
at the lovely Garden of Allah Hotel send you their best wishes. We
have not yet run out of starlets. Fingers crossed. Some day they may
become scarce—wartime rationing and all that. But so far so good.
And there's still plenty of gin for martinis. And speaking of martinis,
stay dry!*

Cheers, Hobey

Quite a lot of news, as usual. The Garden of Allah was a Hollywood frat
house hotel and the semi-permanent home of writers and actors. I lived
there, too, before the war. It was no place for your maiden aunt, but I liked
it. Mostly for that reason. Well, it would be a long time before I saw it
again. Hobey's girlfriend, Hedda Gabler (real name "Betty Something"),
lived there, too. She wrote the Miss Lonelyhearts advice column for a
local LA paper. She had an almost unique lack of empathy and could
read and answer pathetic, and even tragic letters from her readers and

not ever give any of them a second thought. Her advice was useless and in this case actually harmful, but that wasn't the point of her column; the point was to print the pathetic letters and so give readers of the paper a renewed sense that, although their lives might be dreary and meaningless, there were other people out there who were even worse off. As a result, it was a popular column. No surprise about that. The new Bogart movie sounded like it might be good. Ironically, there had been at least one beautiful woman like Bergman in the real Casablanca, when I was there. Amanda. But her eyes never filled with tears under any circumstances. And she'd never make you think of running away from home to join her in a lovers' dream—not because she wasn't as desirable as Bergman. She was. But even an incurable romantic like Hobey would know it would never end well. If there was any running away to do, Amanda would be the one doing it. I knew that for a fact. She'd already run off from me twice, both times after having shot a guy. She was a spy, but as I said, it was an ongoing mystery to me which side she was working for. Could be both, knowing her.

Then thinking about the Bogart movie, I wondered if Hollywood had somehow gotten a hint about Operation Torch. It was possible. Could such a gigantic operation really be kept secret? Besides, the studio moguls had plenty of access to Washington. Campaign contributions bought answered phone calls and inside information. And if so, the studio publicity boys would be presented with a potential bonanza. Knowing them, they'd wait to see if the invasion was a success. If it turned out to be a bloody debacle, the studios would put the Bogart picture on the shelf next to Theda Bara's greatest hits, and it would never be heard of again. But if Torch went well? It would be box office gold, because the name Casablanca would be spread all over the front pages. Well, time would tell. And I had the rueful thought that I'd be there to hear its telling.

By way of reorienting myself after that thought, I took out Martha's letter again. It certainly smelled good. I was suddenly transported back to a private beach in Cuba, where we spent an evening and a night wrapped in a sleeping bag. The sensation reminded me of that French scribbler who was so inspired by the taste of a cookie that he wrote some very long books. The out-of-work or washed-up actors who teach acting in Hollywood call this sort of thing "sense memory," or something like that.

My orders gave me a week to get to Norfolk, so there would be time to stop in New York and see if Martha was there. It was unlikely, I suppose, but worth a try. I had thought about writing to her in Havana—she had a private post office box there. But by the time the letter got there either she'd be gone, or I'd have to leave New York for Norfolk and points beyond before she could get there. So I decided just to chance it. She would either be in New York, or she wouldn't.

She wasn't. Our paths had almost crossed in midair. I called her editor at *Collier's* magazine and asked if she was in town, by any chance.

"Oh," he said. "You just missed her. Are you one of her colleagues?"

That's one word for it, I thought.

"No. Just a friend. Where's she headed?"

"London. And from there, who can say? Wherever the story leads. You know how she is, I assume."

Yes. I did. And because I did, I was disappointed. But it had been a long shot, at best.

"If you want to write to her you can use the APO address. She's fully accredited, and the Army will make sure she gets her mail, eventually. Are you familiar with that process?"

"Yes." APO—Army Post Office. "Thanks."

More disappointed than I thought I'd be, I walked over to the Princeton Club on Park Avenue. As a proud graduate of Old Nassau, Hobey maintained his membership there and long ago had given me a guest card. I didn't know if they'd still honor it, but they did. I suppose it helped that I was in uniform and had a few ribbons displayed. I went into the bar. It was oak paneled and had a stone plaque in the floor of the entrance. It said, "Where women cease from troubling and the wicked are at rest." Personally, I could have used a little troubling just then. Martha or Amanda? Either one would have been welcome. But there was no prospect of that, so I settled for a martini.

"Very dry," I said to the bartender, in Hobey's honor. I signed the check with Hobey's membership number. Someday he'd get around to paying.

I had another one and then strolled uptown to Central Park. It was a perfect fall day, sunny and cool, and for a moment the city looked like a place you could actually stand to live in. The autumn leaves were blowing around the outskirts of the park, and I went in and wandered around for a while. What was the song Martha talked about? "Autumn in New York"? I liked that one, too. I looked around to see if there were any lovers on park benches, like there were in the song. But there weren't. There was only a sad old guy feeding pigeons. I watched him for a while. It was not a scene to inspire joie de vivre. Were he and the dingy birds a metaphor? Some outer reflection of my lonely mood or of life, in general? Not really. He was just some guy I was glad wasn't me. Besides, who said he was sad? Maybe he was just getting away from home for an hour or two of peace and quiet. Or maybe he was a dentist on his coffee break. Then I remembered the song line about "*Dreamers with empty hands, may sigh for exotic lands.*" Maybe so. But I wasn't sighing for any of that. I'd be traveling to exotic lands soon enough, and when I got there I'd probably wish I was back in Central Park sitting next to the old guy and the pigeons—especially if the bastards in Casablanca started shooting at us. Then I thought, not for the first time, it really was too bad I had missed seeing Martha. Making out on a park bench and then going to a nearby hotel to get serious? Now you're talking. No empty hands for those dreamers. She certainly did smell good all the time. Tabu? Taboo? Autumn in New York? Well, maybe next year.

I went over to the Plaza Hotel and had another martini in the Oak Bar. They make a good one. Later that afternoon I caught a C47 transport to Norfolk.

CHAPTER FOUR

NORFOLK HARBOR AND THE DOCKS AND MOORINGS AROUND NEWPORT News and Portsmouth were crammed with shipping. Every one of the ships showed signs of last-minute activity—loading of stores, troops in ranks on the docks, standing there with their duffels and weapons, vehicles being lifted onboard—jeeps, tanks, heavy trucks, and pieces of artillery. Almost all the ships were Navy vessels, but there were also a few civilian transports that had been hired to fill out the requirements of the invasion. Civilians like the *Carlota*.

To anyone, friend or foe, who might be watching, it was obvious that something big was in the works. And I wondered how it was possible to keep the destination secret. Frankly, I didn't see how it could be done, although secrecy was important to the success of the plan. If we could arrive off the coast of North Africa and give the French little or no time to decide whether to fight or not, they may simply decide to say *c'est la vie* and *"Beinvenue mes amis, you are just in time for croissants."* But if they knew we were coming, they'd have time to argue among themselves, and they might decide that French honor required them to put up some sort of fight. After all, we were coming uninvited, and in force, to French territory. I also wondered what kind of disinformation we had put out. I personally knew the story we had spread about the Rhône River and the invasion of southern France. No doubt there were other schemes and false scents being floated toward Vichy and Berlin. I hoped so, at any rate. But this was one huge fleet being assembled, with thousands of troops loading aboard dozens of transports that were protected by dozens of warships. It was impossible to believe that there weren't at least a few German agents in the vicinity—maybe even a U boat watching from just off the coast. And it was equally impossible to believe that they couldn't see that this *might be* an invasion fleet and not just a convoy of men and materiel on the way to England. And if it was an invasion fleet, how many possible destinations could there be? Not all that many, when you stopped to think about it. And wasn't there some midlevel staff officer somewhere working on the plan during the day and sleeping with a possible Mata Hari at night? And couldn't she get a hint or two of what was going on? All over the country there were posters saying, "Loose Lips Sink Ships." Well, there were plenty of ships in Norfolk just then. Could they, *would* they, make it across to North Africa before the enemy got wind of it? It was a long shot, like this whole operation.

I found the *Carlota* at the Naval Supply Depot in Norfolk. All available dock space there was taken up by some sort of vessel, loading either supplies or men. *Carlota* was listing slightly from the weight of her rigged-out booms and cargo nets. Navy and civilian stevedores were loading crates of munitions and fifty-gallon drums of aviation fuel into the massive nets that were then swung over on to *Carlota*'s decks and lowered into her open holds. The markings on her waterline indicated that she was drawing sixteen feet of water, and she was still taking on cargo. I remembered Bunny saying that the maximum draft of a ship going up the Sebou River would be around seventeen feet. So *Carlota* was getting close.

Her crewmen were a scurvy-looking bunch of mixed races. *Carlota* was not much handsomer. She was about 200 feet long, with a single smoke stack and a black hull that had turned gray from age or weather, or both. Here and there on her hull were patches of red lead paint, put there either to replace, or more likely disguise, the rust. Her superstructure had been white once, but it too had faded and was now uniformly dingy. Her decks were littered with ropes and gear and crates of supplies waiting to be shifted into storage. Men were shouting in different languages, and the only lingua franca was intense and creative profanity.

There was a tall, blond man supervising the loading. He was wearing a white turtleneck sweater, dark pants, and a white officer's hat. Youthful and good-looking, he was straight out of central casting. Flynn? He looked more like an Errol than an Elmer.

"Captain Flynn?" I shouted.

He smiled and waved in a friendly way. I walked up the gangway.

"I'm first mate," he said. "Name's Timmons. I suppose you're our naval fellow. Welcome aboard."

"Fitzhugh."

We shook hands, and it seemed to me this was a good start. Timmons was a Brit with one of those regional accents that Henry Higgins could identify, but I couldn't. I learned later that he was new to the ship. The original first mate was in the local hospital. Timmons was a last-minute replacement.

"Ugly brute, isn't she?" he said, pleasantly.

I suppose he read the obvious into the way I was looking around. But he said this with a smile and a trace of affection for the ship that seemed ready to sink alongside the dock, both from the weight of her cargo and from simple old age and fatigue. Landsmen and civilians tend to think of ships as they are in paintings, or as they look from a distance. And my Navy captain, Model T, says that ships are often named after women, because they are all beautiful, even the ugly ones. But he's prejudiced. In reality, many cargo ships are simply seagoing factories made of unromantic steel and iron, and they smell of fuel oil and lubricants and of men without women. They're noisy from clanking engines and ugly from the constant need to keep them afloat and fight off the incessant rust attacks and wage the unwinnable battle against the sea and the weather. To merchant crews, the vessels are nothing more than work places, and they apparently care nothing about aesthetics—unlike any naval officer worth his salt. Merchant ships by and large are floating, slow moving, noisy warehouses, and when they are finally sold for scrap, no one sheds a tear. Not many, anyway. Most merchant ships are as different from a perfectly maintained Navy ship as a peasant is different from a prince. Or rather, a princess. Unlike the ugly duckling that turns into a swan, most tramp steamers start out as ugly ducklings and grow into even uglier ducks, as age and the elements do their worst. Which is always more than enough to do the job.

"Past her prime, maybe?" I said, trying to soften things.

"A diplomat! Yes, that's better. Or perhaps 'Best viewed from afar.'"

"Diplomat" was the operative word. I was in a strange position vis-á-vis the captain and crew. My orders were clear—I was to consider myself a co-captain of this ship, and I was there to see that all fleet orders issued to the ship, the officers and crew were carried out. If I had to use my armed sailors to enforce orders, then I was to do it. If necessary, I was to take over the ship. On the other hand, a captain of a ship—even the most woebegone tramp steamer—is traditionally considered morally and legally as God's representative on earth. The Stuarts' or Bourbons' belief in the divine right of kings was nothing compared to a captain's belief in his own authority. So diplomacy on my part would be in order. Force was a last resort. I didn't know whether the officers and crew of the *Carlota* knew any of this, and unless it became critical for them to learn it, I was happy enough to keep my orders to myself and play the role of a friendly colleague—respectful, but outside the chain of command and only there to lend any professional help that might be required. And as far as the civilian crew was concerned, my men were there primarily to man the gun. The fact that they would be wearing side arms at all times could be marked down to naval melodramatics.

I glanced toward the bow. The three-inch fifty gun I had been prom-ised was there all right, but it was as elderly as its surroundings. Naval guns in turrets are handsome, but standing alone with their mechanical workings exposed, they are less so. You see quite clearly that they, too, are machines. Still, aesthetics aside, I was glad to see the gun. It wasn't much, but it was better than nothing, and my men were familiar with the type. We had a similar gun on the *Nameless*, and last year had done some serious damage to a secret German fuel dump in Cuba. Pointed properly, the gun could do its job against shore targets or a U boat. But the only aircraft it could hope to worry was a blimp. Cranking the elevation and bearing by hand made it impossible to take aim at even the slowest air-plane, if it flew any kind of evasive maneuver.

"Any of my men show up yet, Mr. Timmons?" I said.

"Your men? No. Not yet."

"How about a Frenchman named Rene Malevergne. I think he's supposed to travel with us."

"Yes, he's here, somewhere. The skipper'll be able to fill you in. He's in his sea cabin, just aft of the pilot house. Can't miss it. Just up that ladder to the bridge."

"Thanks."

I clanked up the ladder to the pilot house and found the captain's sea cabin easily enough. The captain used this as a place to sleep while underway. He could be close to the pilot house in case of emergencies. I'm sure he also had a more comfortable cabin in the area where *Carlota* housed her civilian passengers, when the ship was traveling between the US and South America.

There was no door, just a curtain over the opening. I knocked on the bulkhead.

"Yes?"

"Lieutenant Fitzhugh, reporting, sir."

"Ah. Good. Come in. We've been expecting you."

Unlike the first mate, Captain Flynn was not from central casting. He hardly looked like someone who could survive a shootout with banditos. But apparently he had proved once again that looks can be deceiving, though I've also learned that looks can now and then tell you something worth knowing. Captain Flynn was egg shaped and balding, and he wore thick glasses. His khaki "uniform" was limp with wear, and he had his pants hitched up and buckled over his paunch, so that there was only a few buttons of shirt front showing. He had a pale pencil moustache that you had to look twice to notice, and a ruddy complexion, most likely from exposure. He was not very tall—maybe five and a half feet, in his shoes. But like the first mate, he seemed friendly enough. He stood up and shook hands with me, and he seemed genuinely glad to see me.

"Welcome aboard."

"Thank you, Captain. I'm happy to be here."

"Really? Well, I'm pleased to hear it. Not everyone would be. Take a pew."

The cabin was Spartan—a metal desk, metal cot with a thin mattress, a metal locker for clothes, and one extra metal chair. Everything was painted hospital green. The deck was green linoleum. The only bright spot was a framed eight-by-ten photo on the desk, amid a scattering of official-looking papers. The picture was of a gorgeous woman, smiling with a trace of roguishness. The image didn't fit with the surroundings, and she looked all the more spectacular, because of that. Flynn saw me notice her.

"Beautiful isn't she?"

"Very."

"Brightens up my day every time I look at her."

I wondered—could she be his wife? Girlfriend? It seemed hardly possible, but I had spent enough time around beautiful women in Hollywood to know that there is absolutely no way to predict what a woman will find appealing in a man. A stunning blonde will be drawn to a garden gnome, and it's not always because the gnome has a lot of money. One of the most glamorous women I knew doted on a guy who looked like Gabby Hayes and was always flat broke, because he was a lousy poker player. And the word was his pecker was no more than average. So the two most common explanations didn't apply. Sometimes, things make no sense.

"She is my dream girl," Flynn said, happily.

"I can well believe it. Is she your wife?" I said.

"My wife? Oh, no. That picture came with the frame."

"Oh."

"I call her Beatrice," he said, "though that's probably not her real name."

"Pretty name." I thought about saying something clever about Dante's Beatrice, but didn't. No one likes a smart ass, as my skipper liked to say.

The only other unusual thing in the cabin, aside maybe from the captain, was a parrot that was perched on a metal coat rack in the corner. The bird eyed me as if trying to decide whether to attack.

"Don't mind him," said Flynn. "He doesn't like anyone, but he's harmless. I leave him loose in the hopes that one day he'll fly away and not come back. But I've had him five years, and he hasn't left yet. I call it a failure of imagination on his part. He must know he's not wanted, but still he stays. Some people are like that, too. No doubt you've noticed that."

"Yes. Smart birds, though. At least that's what I've heard. Does he talk a lot?"

"Never says a word. Silent as the tomb. I bought him in Hong Kong from a Chinaman who swore the bird could recite the Lord's Prayer, King James Version, and a Shakespeare sonnet to boot—'Shall I compare thee to a bleedin' summer's day.' That one. I expect you know it."

"Yes. But not by heart." And not that version.

"He doesn't either, apparently. Well, that was five years ago, and he hasn't opened his beak since then on any subject. I suppose I shouldn't complain, because he only cost me five Hong Kong dollars and a bottle of rum."

"I didn't think the Chinese liked rum."

"They don't as a rule. But this one was living with a white Russian woman. Her standards had bottomed out considerably since the revolution. She had to settle for rum and a Chinese boyfriend, because there wasn't a handy Cossack and no vodka, other than the stuff they made in Macao, which tastes like antifreeze. Ever tried it?"

"No."

"Only a desperate Russian peasant will drink it. But she was an aristocrat. Wouldn't touch it. Anyway, the bird didn't cost much. Even so, it rankles whenever I think about being cheated. But when you buy a parrot from a Chinaman, you've got to expect that sort of thing."

"Good to know. What's his name?"

"The parrot? They told me it was Cato, but he doesn't answer to that, or anything else."

"You were misinformed."

"Yes. That's one word for it. Well, I was younger then. But not much. I tried to give him away one time, but he flew back to me. Must have some homing pigeon in his background. Not surprising. Lots of half castes in the Orient."

I wondered—was Captain Flynn was putting me on? He told his story with a straight face, but I thought I could see a glimmer of humor behind his thick glasses. I had run into quite a few of these veteran merchant captains. They seemed to fall into two categories—the ones who were silent and gloomy from the loneliness of command, and the ones who were friendly and tellers of tall tales, for much the same reason. I had also met a few Aussie naval officers. To a man, they were fun loving and full of stories, and I had yet to meet one I didn't like. I began to think that maybe Captain Flynn would be no different. I hoped so. Come to think of it, he may have been pulling my leg about Beatrice, too. Maybe that's why looking at her made him feel good. She was a joke on many levels, as well as being a harmless fantasy.

"When we finish this trip," he said, "I'm going to give Cato to an old auntie of mine. She lives in London. She was from the branch of the family that stayed in England, when the other branch moved to Austra-lia. They didn't want to, but they didn't have any choice. She's deaf and won't know whether Cato's talking to her on not. She can read lips, but that won't help with a parrot. But this way she can imagine he's saying whatever she wants. So they'll always agree. She's a fundamentalist and will appreciate his piety."

"In that case, maybe you should tell her he knows a few Psalms, too."

He looked at me and grinned.

"Good idea. Once she gets attached to him, maybe she can keep him from following me. I haven't seen her in a while, but she writes to me regularly. Keeps me informed about news in England. Ask me about the rising cost of marmalade, and I can tell you everything you need to know. Well, what do you think of *Carlota*?"

"I haven't seen much of her, yet."

"Well, when you do, you'll see she ain't much to look at. She's like an old lady with a wooden leg—she lists a bit and she's not going to win any races, but she still gets around. I don't suppose you understand the significance of her name."

"Not really."

"No? You'll find this interesting. Carlota was a real person—a Bel-gian. She was empress of Mexico, for a brief time. If you're wondering how she got that job, it was a case of being in the right place at the right time, although things didn't work out so well in the end, and she lost her mind, which was careless. It all started when the French lent Mexico some money—this was back in 1860 or thereabouts. The Mexicans were happy about it at first, but after they spent it all, they decided that they'd rather not pay it back. So the French sent an army to collect, and they tossed out the deadbeat Mexican government and installed a guy named Archduke Maximillian as emperor. 'Archduke' wasn't his first name, you understand. That was his Austrian title. He wasn't doing anything else at the time and was available. What's more, the French figured he'd be more agreeable about paying back the loan. He was the younger brother of the Austrian emperor, you see. Napoleon the Third was running things in France, so he figured they'd all be able to work things out, the three all being emperors and somehow related. Probably played cards together. Anyway, Maximillian was married to Carlota. She went by Charlotte at the time of her marriage, when Maximillian was still just an archduke, and only changed her name when she became a Mexican. Like I said, up till then she'd been a Belgian, like Hercule Poirot. The couple apparently liked each other well enough and got along with the upper-class Mexicans, but not with the peasants. They didn't want any royalty and didn't like the French army riding around the country sticking the rebels with lances. This was during your American Civil War, you understand, so the French were able to pull this off without you Yanks noticing or saying anything about the Monroe Doctrine. I expect you've heard of that."

"Yes, sir."

"Well, after a while, the French got tired of the expense of keeping their army in Mexico and pulled out, leaving Maximillian to his own devices."

"Did the French get their money?"

"I imagine they did, by hook or by crook, if you follow me. I also imagine most of the officers went home with more than just a case of the trots to remember Mexico by. But when the French pulled out, things got more comfortable for the Mexican rebels, under this fellow Juarez."

"I've heard of him."

"I'm not surprised. Named after a Mexican town, I believe. Up till then, Juarez and his boys had been stuck in the mountains living off tortillas and beans. But they rose up and overthrew Maximillian's crowd and stood him against a wall, and that was the end of Maximillian, after they shot him. By all accounts he took it like a man, even though to look at him you wouldn't expect much. When Juarez viewed the body, his only comment was that Max had short legs. Not much of an epitaph for an emperor. Anyway, while all this was going on, Carlota was in Europe trying to borrow some money and not succeeding and trying to convince her various relatives that they ought to help Maximillian before things got out of hand, which they already had, although she didn't know it. And sometime during her spare time, Carlota had an affair with a Belgian officer, and the result of that will surprise you."

"Really?"

"It was none other than the French General Weygand—the very same one who's in North Africa now doing his best to get along with the Germans. Now and then he pops up in Vichy, too."

"That *is* interesting."

Funny how history delivers these little ironies. We were sitting aboard a bucket named *Carlota*, getting ready to leave for the current home of the original Carlota's love child, a possible enemy. I didn't say anything about it to Captain Flynn, though. I was pretty sure he and the other skippers, for that matter, hadn't been told yet where they were going. Orders would be issued once the fleet was at sea. Most of the rumors said we were a convoy taking troops and their supplies to England, and it was just as well to let those rumors float.

"When was he born? Weygand."

"Somewhere around 1867. So he's getting along in years, but bastards live a long time, as a rule. Like parrots. He can't seem to make up his mind which side he's on. Of course, with French politics there are always more than two sides. That way, changing your mind doesn't seem so obvious or unusual. Just a slight slide right or left. 'Shuffle ball change' they call it in tap dancing. My old mother made me take dancing lessons when I was a nipper. Scarred me for life, psychologically. Had to run away from home and go to sea to escape the shame of it."

I could see he was waiting for me to respond. I was used to this sort of thing. My skipper, Model T, was a great teller of stories, too, and appreciated a straight man.

"How old were you when you left?"

"Almost twenty-five."

"Well, it's a colorful story," I said. "The one about Carlota, I mean."

"Yes, it is, although some people say the ship's not named after the crazy Empress. They say it's named for the owner's college sweetheart."

"Which do you believe?"

"Well, I prefer the first story. Has more human interest. Besides, I've met the ship's owner. I doubt he ever had a college sweetheart. Not one named Carlota, anyway."

"Then I'll follow your lead, Captain."

"Good. We'll get along just fine. So, I understand that you're here to watch over the naval guard and protect us from mutiny and pirates."

"Yes, sir. Your first mate told me my men haven't arrived yet. Have you had any word about them?"

"No, but I expect they'll show up soon. They'd better, because we're sailing day after tomorrow."

"How about the Frenchman, Rene Malevergne? Your first mate told me he's turned up."

"Yes. He's in his cabin on the first class deck. Nice fella. You'll be more or less right next door. I think he's there now, if you want to say hello."

"Good idea."

"Well, I'm glad to have you with us. Maybe you and your boys can pot us a U boat."

"We'll give it a rip, if they're dumb enough to surface."

"Well, let's hope they are. I wouldn't want to have to dodge a torpedo. The old *Carlota*'s been through a lot, like her namesake. She's not as nimble as she used to be. And there are spots on her bottom that you wouldn't want to examine too closely."

I considered making a joke about the real Carlota's bottom, but decided against it. Too obvious.

Chapter Five

I WENT DOWN ONE DECK TO THE FIRST CLASS CABINS AND FOUND THE one I'd been assigned to. The cabin décor had a tropical feel, which I suppose was appropriate given *Carlota*'s previous life as a banana boat. The furniture reminded me of those Bob Hope–Bing Crosby movies when Dorothy Lamour shows up in a flowered sarong. But it was not the curvaceous Dorothy Lamour of the present day, but the Dorothy Lamour of forty years in the future, for the furniture pillows and cushions that had once been plump and firm were now flattened and sagging from the press of time and countless passengers, and the flowered patterns on the chair cushions were faded into pale blotches. Everything smelled of mildew—the ever-present perfume of the tropics. I thought the rattan furniture and a straw rug on the deck would make a fine fire, if we ever ran into the enemy or had an accident. But on the other hand, if there ever was a fire on *Carlota*, flammable furniture and rugs would be the least of our worries.

There was a sink on the bulkhead and a private head—a luxury for a sailor. The bed mattress was no younger than the rest of the furniture, and when I tossed my sea bag on it, I could hear the springs complaining. But it would be all right. I'd slept in worse places, and not all that long ago. There was one porthole, and I opened it to let some Tidewater air into the cabin. It was damp, too, but a fresher damp.

Speaking of Dorothy Lamour—I met her one time at a party in Hollywood. She seemed like a nice lady. Her real name was Mary Slaton, but of course a change of names was not unusual in that town. In the movie business, everyone starts out as someone else. After all, "what's in a name?" One of the up-and-coming cowboy stars had a horse named

"Blanco." The horse's real name was "Ned." The studio changed it, because "Hi Ho, Blanco" sounds a lot more dramatic than "Hi Ho, Ned." Most of the studio executives were uneducated hustlers, but they had a nose for what sells. When it came to the box office, they usually knew what they were doing.

I went down the passageway to Rene Malevergne's cabin and knocked on the door.

"*Entrez.*" I went in.

I had met Rene in London, after we both had escaped the clutches of the Vichy police and the Gestapo in Morocco. He knew my story, and I knew most of his.

"Ah, Lieutenant," he said pleasantly. "The famous duck! We meet again."

"I think you mean to say 'the famous decoy.'"

"Truly? Oh. Yes. Now that I think of it, that is correct. 'Decoy.' Well, whatever you call it, it worked famously. The police followed you, and while they were looking one way, I went the other. *Parfait!* And we are both here now. *Bon!* I congratulate ourselves. Yes?"

"Yes."

Rene was about five-four and stocky. Somewhat more than forty, he had been in the French navy during the First War and had settled in Morocco afterward and become the head pilot on the Sebou River. Before the OSS recruited him and then spirited him out of Morocco, he had been arrested by the Vichy police and sent to France for trial. He was accused of planning to help forty Belgian airman escape by ship to England. They had been stranded in Morocco after the French surrender. A spy had denounced the plotters, and Rene had spent several months in a variety of Moroccan and French prisons before being unaccountably acquitted by a military tribunal. His defense was the partial truth that he was only a river pilot, and his responsibility was to guide ships in and out of the river all the way to Port Lyautey and back, but it was not his job to know about the cargo, human or otherwise. He also denounced the informant as unreliable, and there was some sentiment among the judges that their spy was in fact an unreliable human cockroach, and Rene was acquitted. But his six months or so of doing hard time in French colonial prisons had left him understandably bitter. Besides, he had no sympathy for the collaborationist French and had willingly gone along with the OSS ideas about helping with the Sebou River attack. This was all the more courageous, because he was married and had two sons, and they lived in the river town of Mehdia, which was on the south bank of the Sebou at the mouth and only just down from the ancient Portuguese fort called the Kasbah. The Portuguese had built the fort two centuries ago, but it still was a looming menace over the river. The French had garrisoned it, and its guns would be a problem for anyone trying to force their way upriver to Port Lyautey, twelve miles away. The fact that his home and the town of Mehdia might be in the firing line if the French resisted our invasion worried Rene, of course, but he still volunteered for the mission. He was the best sort of French patriot. And a pleasant man, to boot. I was looking forward to our voyage together and delivering the *Carlota* and Rene to the Sebou River mouth. At that point I would rejoin my ship, the PC 475, also known as the *Nameless*.

There was only one thing—when I came into his room, Rene was packing.

"Are you moving to another room?" I said, indicating his zipped-up suitcase.

"*Alors*, yes. In a manner of speaking. And my new room is on another ship. You are just in time to say goodbye. I have received orders this morning to transfer to the *Susan B. Anthony*. A transport."

"Really? Why?"

He shrugged as only a Frenchman can.

"Who can say? Orders. But I think it is a good omen. I believe that the real Susan B. Anthony is a famous beauty and a star of the cinema. I believe I saw her most recent film. An exquisite bosom. And such eyes! She is perfect in the role of courtesan. *Charmante*. Do you know her?"

"Not personally."

"But you know her work?"

"I've read something about it, yes."

"She is like that picture Captain Flynn has of his beautiful mistress, Beatrice. A dream."

"Yes. That's about it."

"Ah, well. A man can love his wife and family and still imagine the pleasures of another woman, is it not? With luck and discretion, he can do more than just imagine. Eh?"

"Yes. With luck and discretion."

"I agree. Well, I am sorry we will not be traveling together, *mon ami*, but it is a short voyage, if all goes well. Time will pass. And I will see you on the other side, *n'est ce pas?*"

There was no sense explaining that "on the other side" had a different meaning in English idiom, just as there was no sense puncturing Rene's illusions about Susan B. Anthony. Besides, maybe there really was another Susan B. Anthony, though I doubted it. Even the Hollywood studio flaks would not be dumb enough to name an up and coming starlet after the original. I'd seen photos of her, and she did not seem to match Rene's vision. Nor did I think *charmante* was the best possible adjective. So I nodded and smiled and helped him carry his gear to the main deck and shook his hand and bid him bon voyage. Then I went back to my room to think about things.

Being surprised about a sudden change in orders is a mug's game. Changes happen all the time. Who was the Greek who nattered on about life as a flowing stream? Starts with an H. It certainly applied to the Navy. Still, I wondered what this meant to me. Nothing, I guess. My job was to make sure the *Carlota* made the trip on schedule and arrived at the mouth of the Sebou in time to play her part in the upstream attack. I hadn't been given any responsibility for Rene. Maybe there were better facilities on the Anthony, better ways to plan for the river passage, and for that reason they transferred him off *Carlota*. Maybe it was a matter of security. After all, Rene knew more about the plans for the coming attack than almost all of the officers and men who would be asked to make it. Well, whatever the reason for his transfer, I wouldn't find it out till it was all over. If then. But I guess it didn't really matter.

Later that afternoon the Fubars arrived. They were lined up on the main deck, out of the way of the loading that was beginning to wind down. They were standing at elaborate attention and grinning when I came up on deck to meet them. They saluted, and I returned it.

"Fubars, reporting, sir," said Williams the gunner's mate first class and senior enlisted man.

"You're late," I said. I was even more glad to see them than I thought I'd be.

"Fubar time, sir," he said. "On the dot."

They were all in their dress blues and looked immaculate. Even their trademark Fubar mustaches were trimmed and seamanlike. They grew them as a badge of their special position on the ship—the landing party, the boarding party, and the repel boarders party, all wrapped in one. Most looked reasonably menacing except Smithers, whose blond fuzz looked like it could be wiped away the next time he blew his nose. We had lost two of the original gang during the bombing attack. I had to write those letters. But they had been replaced by two volunteers. The men had been on the *Nameless* from the beginning, so I knew them and their quality. Both were good men and I was glad to have them on the team. One went by Pancho, because he looked a little like a character in a Cisco Kid movie. The other went by Lefty, not because he was left-handed. He wasn't. But because he liked the sound of it. Pancho and Lefty were both from the Deck Department on the *Nameless* and were used to each other. It was customary for an officer to call enlisted men by their last names, but in a small ship in wartime, protocol could sometimes slip and allow the use of nicknames. So it was with Pancho and Lefty, my new Fubars.

"At ease," I said. I grinned at them and told them sincerely how glad I was to see them.

"We're glad to be here, too, Mister Fitzhugh," said Otto, who was a signalman. "Beats sitting around Scotland waiting for the yardbirds to finish putting *Nameless* back together."

"And worrying whether the bastards would go on strike," said Pancho. I understood what he meant. The British unions unaccountably threatened to strike if things weren't going their way, but they wouldn't let our men work in their place, either. This, with a war going on. It was hard to believe.

"And drinking warm beer," said Smithers, who wasn't old enough to drink any kind of beer. Not here, anyway. He had been our only casualty last year in our landing party action against the German U boat base in

Cuba. His arm had been injured after the huge explosion of the ammunition dump we'd detonated. The blast broke off a tree branch that landed on his arm.

"I see you got your purple heart, Smithers." He was wearing the ribbon.

"Yes, sir. The ladies like it. Best broken arm I ever got. Still aches sometimes, but I don't care."

"Pussy," said Reynolds, our quartermaster third class, trumpet player and music critic. "I've been hurt worse teaching Scottish girls the jitterbug."

"Not surprising, the way you dance," said Otto.

"You know what they wear under their kilts, sir? Nothing. Toward the end of the night at those canteen dances, they'll call you over to a dark corner, pull up that kilt and say 'Straight up the middle, Jimmy.'"

"That's right, sir," said Otto. "They call all of us 'Jimmy.'"

"Makes you wonder what their mothers would say," said Williams, who, at thirty, was the old man of the group and was said to have a wife.

"I thought only the men wore kilts," I said.

"Well, you know, sir. It gets dark over there after curfew."

"Where've you been, sir?" said Otto. "We heard stories, but you know how those are."

"I was on a special assignment. Once we're underway and out of sight of land, I'll tell you about it."

"Did you get laid, sir?"

"Constantly. Triplets."

"All at the same time?"

"Yes. There were some nights I almost couldn't handle them."

They all nodded sagely, as if to say they'd had similar problems, themselves. Most of them knew I was kidding, of course, except for maybe Smithers. On the other hand, they all also knew I had spent the last few years before the war as a PI in Hollywood, and stories of my cavorting with the stars and starlets circulated freely aboard *Nameless*. Some of it was true, but not much. Still, I knew that sort of thing didn't hurt my reputation with the men, so I let most of it pass without comment or false modesty.

"What are we doing here, sir?"

"We're taking this bucket across the Atlantic along with the rest of the fleet. The crew is all civilians, and we're the naval armed guard. This afternoon we'll draw small arms from Supply, and we'll wear side arms at all times. We've got one three-inch fifty to operate in case of enemy action, so, Williams, make it your first order of business to check that gun and survey the ammunition in the magazine."

"Aye, aye, sir."

"Otto, you and the others go on over to Supply and draw our weapons and ammunition. Here's a list of what we'll want. I've made out the requisition, and alerted them that you'll be coming, so there won't be any problem."

"Do we bunk in crew quarters, sir?"

"Hell, no. I was afraid you guys might get corrupted by these civilians—learn to play cards and cuss. So I've arranged cabins for you on the passenger deck."

"Bugger!" said Reynolds with appreciation. He had spent his time in Britain picking up the lingo while picking up the girls. "A blooming pleasure cruise! All we need now is to hear is we're carrying cases of Scotch and decent American beer!"

"Not quite," I said. "We're loaded up with ammunition and Av gas."

That sobered them, but only momentarily. They were sailors and therefore knew there was always a hitch, somewhere. Too good to be true was always too good to be true. It was an immutable law and just about the only one they believed in, to a man. But because they were sailors, they couldn't be depressed for more than a minute. Two at the most.

"Bloody hell," said Reynolds, cheerfully. "A blooming floating bomb. Be careful where you toss your fags, mates."

"As to that," I said, "the smoking lamp is out throughout the ship and for the duration of the voyage—except in your cabins. You'll double up, so that you can keep an eye on each other and make sure no one falls asleep with a Lucky Strike burning. Smithers, have you taken up smoking yet?"

"No, sir. I tried it once but didn't like it."

"That's what she said," said Otto.

"Will we be standing underway watch, sir?"

"Yes. But only at the gun. Two-man watches, round the clock. That's to make sure the gun stays secure and ready and that none of these civilians tamper with it. I don't think they would, but once you get a good look at them you'll understand why I'm being careful. If we go to general quarters, we'll all be at the gun. Other than that, there'll be no normal underway watches—unless it turns out the crew are useless as lookouts. But we'll be traveling in a huge convoy, so there should be plenty of eyes watching. If things change, we'll adapt. I'll be on the bridge most of the time. Any other questions?"

"What was the names of the triplets?" said Smithers, sincerely.

"Names? Ah, let me think. Oh, yes . . . Maxene, Patty, and LaVerne," I said.

"You mean . . . the Andrews Sisters, sir?" Smithers was agog. "Gosh!"

Reynolds looked at me and smiled slyly. He was a musician in civilian life and once played in a band that accompanied the Andrews Sisters. He didn't like them very much. Their singing was all right but that was about the extent of their appeal, as far as he was concerned. "You look at them from behind for long enough and the bloom comes off the petunia," he'd said. "And one of them had really bad breath."

"I'd of thought you could do better than that, sir," he said.

"There's a war on, Reynolds," I said. "We all have to make sacrifices and do the best we can."

"Aye, aye, sir."

My skipper on the *Nameless* used to sit on his chair on the bridge with a cup of coffee and a cigar, and he'd watch the men going about their morning duties, and he'd look out at the horizon with the sky reaching down to the sea and he'd say to me, "You know, Riley, there's no place on earth I'd rather be than right here." I understood what he was talking about. I didn't always feel that way, but I did a lot of the time. And even though we were on board the slow, rusted *Carlota*, instead of the sleek and spotless *Nameless*, it was still good to be back.

CHAPTER SIX

"DRUNKENNESS AND FORNICATION," SAID TIMMONS, WITH A BROAD grin. "That's what got me sent down, chucked out. Fornication with a woman, I hasten to add."

"The best kind," I said.

"Yes. Her name was Sally. She was a buxom barmaid at the local pub. Lovely girl. She had a gap between her two front teeth—you know what that signifies, I assume. Made a charming whistling sound when she was excited. 'Sally Free and Easy' we lads called her. Someone should write a song about her."

"That would make a good title," I said.

"Yes. Funnily enough, her last name was actually 'Free.' We just added 'And Easy.'"

We were on the bridge of the *Carlota*, underway in slow pursuit of the convoy. We had been the last to get underway, for reasons best known to the admiral's staff when they issued the sailing orders. That was all right as far as I was concerned. We'd catch up to the main body soon enough. I wasn't at all sure how adept the *Carlota's* crew, meaning Captain Flynn and First Mate Timmons, would be at maintaining station in a convoy. Merchant captains were notoriously independent and traditionally sailed alone, so at the start of the war they had almost no practice in the art of convoy sailing. They only submitted because independent sailing had become too dangerous. In the case of Operation Torch, of course, the very few merchants were under the direct command of the Navy and the Admiral, so they had little choice in the matter. But the convoy was a necessary evil to them and a wearisome exercise in constant watch-keeping to make sure they were staying on station. If they didn't, they would hear it from the flagship. And for reasons of security, our convoy would be tightly bunched—each ship one thousand yards from the ships ahead and behind, one thousand yards from ships to each side. What's more, *Carlota*'s radar was very primitive and unreliable, and radar is very useful—almost critical—in helping you maintain position in a convoy. I hoped our rickety outfit would suffice. Otherwise we'd have to start judging our range the old-fashioned way, which I had learned in officer training and promptly forgotten.

Our assigned position was at the tail end on the outside column, so keeping station would be a little more comfortable without a ship to the starboard side of us. And we would be screened by the destroyers that would cruise around outside the main body. Even so, I was apprehensive. One-thousand-yard intervals sounds like a big distance, but at sea it feels like you're in each other's pockets. Ships do not stop quickly, and they do not turn in tight circles; they need space to do both. And every ship, even ships of the same class, has slightly different handling characteristics. Place two identical ships on the same course, side by side, and order the engine room to set the same speed using the same RPM on the screws, and inevitably one ship will drift ahead or behind, or closer or farther, from the other. When trying to stay at an assigned place relative to each other, the officer on the bridge will have to adjust his course and RPM constantly to stay in the assigned position. Now place a hundred ships in assigned positions relative to each other—most of them with completely different handling characteristics, hull configurations, and power plants—and tell them to stay that way while traversing four thousand miles of ocean in all kinds of weather and sea conditions, and you have a job that requires constant vigilance and skill on the bridge. Merchant ships like the *Carlota* were the least handy of all, and although almost all of the ships in this convoy were Navy vessels and could be expected to be well handled, the few merchant ships were slow and ungainly, and their crews were inexperienced in station keeping. Not one of them had made a voyage across the Atlantic in a convoy. I was afraid that *Carlota* would be the worst of them all. What's more, once in convoy, we would be zigzagging to protect against U boats, while the destroyers and screening warships dashed around the outside and now and then darted between ships in formation, perhaps to follow a sonar contact. Even with experienced ship handlers, zigzagging in a convoy can feel like a Chinese fire drill, and it only takes one mistake, one zig instead of a zag, to cause a collision. The fact that the *Carlota* was much less experienced than our Navy comrades meant that the voyage for us, and for me in particular, was probably going to be a sleepless one. And I was quite sure we were in for ten days or so of harsh messages from the flagship telling us to do a better job of maintaining our position relative to the main body.

But for the moment we were steaming along by ourselves. We were late because the pilot who was assigned to take us through the minefield that guarded the harbor had been slow in getting to us. We put him off just after we cleared the mines, and he went back to Norfolk in the pilot boat. And as we looked for the convoy we saw nothing but empty horizon. There were a few smudges of smoke in their direction, but that was all. But we knew the course, and we knew the coordinates of the rendezvous, so we steamed along the best we could. The rendezvous was the first object, because there were other elements of the Torch invasion fleet coming down from New York. We'd all meet at the designated spot and then head to North Africa together—albeit with sufficient course changes to disguise our true destination, until the last possible moment.

I was on the bridge with the first mate. I could hear Captain Flynn snoring in his sea cabin. He'd been up most of the night fussing about something in the engine room, and Timmons had taken over for him as soon as we cleared the minefield. I was simply an advisor, as far as Timmons knew. That would be my role, I hoped, for the duration of the voyage. I was authorized to take over the ship, as necessary, but of course I hoped that wouldn't happen.

Timmons seemed glad to have someone to talk to. The only other person on the bridge was the helmsman, who was a swarthy-looking Mediterranean who spoke in a thick accent of some kind, but said very little. I was glad that Timmons liked to talk, because I was interested in his professional experience. I needed to know if he was a dependable seaman. I could observe the way he handled himself and the ship, but I was also interested in his background. "Dependability" meant more than being able to handle a ship.

I learned that his father was a country parson on the south coast of England, not far from Southampton. Timmons, whose first name was Nigel, was raised around boats and had been sailing since he was a boy. That was a good sign. "Just messing about in boats," he said. "Nothing quite like it. Do you know the *Wind in the Willows*?"

"Yes, as a matter of fact."

"That's me. Just like Mister Water Rat—never happier than messing about in boats. But the gov'ner, bless him, thought I should have a career of some sort. Law, or something equally dreary, like stock broking in the City. He was dead keen on sending me to public school. I suppose you know that term."

"Yes. I have a friend who went to Eton."

"Really? Very posh, of course. Parsons don't make much money, though, and Papa couldn't afford to send me to any of the best schools. Or even barely decent ones. But I was able to get a scholarship to a dreadful place in Wales. A school called Llanabba. Have you heard of it?"

"No."

"I'm not surprised. Not many have. It was run by an old duffer named Grimes. Very low church—almost a Methodist—and very strict about everything that makes life worth living. Strictly against all of it, you see. He was as grim and gloomy as the Welsh weather. Wore old-fashioned side whiskers. Well, that tells you something right there. But I stuck it out for the guv'nor's sake. Unfortunately, early in my last year, Papa took ill with the flu and passed on to his undoubted reward—and a reunion with Mother. Not the same things. I don't remember her well, but what I do remember, I'd just as soon forget. Terrible of me, I know, but there it is. Anyway, Papa left me two hundred pounds in his will, and I spent some of it on champagne and Sally Free over two glorious weekend days and nights, and in the wee hours of Monday morning I was delivered back to school by two yokels carrying me on a hurdle as a makeshift stretcher. They dumped me outside Grimes' door, thinking it'd be a jolly surprise for Grimes when he greeted the day. And so it was. I was surprised, too, of course, upon waking up on the headmaster's door step. That very day Dr. Grimes expelled me and sent me on my way with some solemn words of pious advice, which I have studiously ignored. I left that gloomy prison with a song in my heart and a rash from Sally and went to sea on the first ship that would take me. That was more than ten years ago now. The rash cleared up and I have worked my way up to first mate by applying myself in ways I never did at school. Not surprising, of course. People are generally good at doing things they like, and not so good at doing things that disgust them, don't you agree?"

"Yes, of course."

"I'm not at all good at buggery, for example."

"Good to know."

"So all's well that ends well. I'm back to messing about in boats, or rather ships, and couldn't be happier."

"Whatever happened to Sally?"

"Oh, nothing. She's still working at the pub. She has a half interest in the place, you see. Smart businesswoman. I heard she had twins not long after I left, but they turned out to be black, so no fingers were pointed at me. She named them Disraeli and Gladstone, because she had an interest in that period of English history. Funny name for girls, but black twins were rather unconventional in that part of Wales, anyway. The father was a merchant sailor down for the weekend from Liverpool, apparently. He disappeared, of course. Sally was a talented gal. She could pump a beer engine with anyone, man or woman, and tell you whatever you wanted to know about the Corn Laws. Still can, I'm sure."

We were out of sight of land, and the day was calm. There were only gentle swells, hardly worthy of the name, and there was a mild haze in the air. The convoy was still ahead. I figured we had another forty or so miles to go before we caught up. That would take a while, because our speed was only a few knots faster than the convoy. Captain Flynn was concerned about overtaxing the engines. I was standing on the wing of the bridge thinking about Martha and wondering where she was and what she was up to. Wherever it was, she would be happy as long as she was on assignment in the middle of whatever action there was, political or military.

Up on the bow two Fubars—Otto and Williams—were lolling by the gun, which was covered over with a tarp to protect its workings and lubrication from the salt air. It was a warm day, and like so many at sea, perfectly peaceful. Even the clanks and hums of the *Carlota's* systems and engine seemed to be subdued. We were making black smoke—always a sign of inefficient fuel use and a red flag to any skipper worth his pay, but no one seemed to care. It struck me of course that smoke was an invitation to any enemies who might be lurking in the area. I was about to say something to Timmons, when I heard a shout from a lookout who was posted in the masthead.

"PERISCOPE! STARBOARD BOW!"

If ever there's a cry that will freeze your blood, it was that one. Only the sight of a dorsal fin circling a swimmer creates a similar emotion. And there was very little difference between them; it was not just metaphorical similarity.

I looked up to where the lookout was pointing and then searched the sea ahead with my binoculars. For a moment I saw nothing, but then all at once there it was—a black stick-like object protruding above the surface and creating a small white wake. God, it was a frightful sight. And it seemed, unfairly, to have arrived too soon. We were hardly beyond the sight of land, just beyond Norfolk and Virginia Beach. There were families and children playing in the sand only an hour so from here. And yet the U boats were here already.

I ran back into the pilot house. Timmons had heard the lookout, too, and was searching with his glasses.

"Call the convoy," I said. "Call the flagship and give them our position. Maybe they've got some planes in the air. They could be here in a few minutes."

Timmons nodded. He seemed under control, but alive to the danger.

"What's the flagship's call sign?" he said. He should have known that. But he didn't.

"Sharetti," I said.

Timmons stepped back to the radio shack that was just behind the pilot house.

"Call Sharetti and tell them we have a U boat sighting," he yelled to the radioman.

"What's our call sign?" said the flustered radioman. And for a moment Timmons looked at him, dumbfounded.

"It's Fatboy, you idiot. Do it."

The radioman picked up the phone and sent his message in clear.

"Sharetti, this is Fatboy-You-Idiot. Sharetti, this is Fatboy-You-Idiot. Over."

"Fatboy, this is Sharetti. Over." Apparently the flagship radioman understood what was going on. I could imagine him grinning. Timmons grabbed the phone from the radioman and said:

"Sharetti, this is Fatboy. We have sighted a periscope off the starboard bow, one thousand yards. Over."

"Roger, Fatboy. What is your position? Over."

Timmons gave our approximate range and bearing from the convoy. "Can you send aircraft? Over."

There was a slight delay while orders were considered and issued.

"Roger, Fatboy. CAP vectoring to you. Over."

Timmons wasn't sure what CAP meant. It stood for Combat Air Patrol. In the convoy, the attack carrier, *Ranger*, would have at least two combat planes in the air at all times, both to scout for enemies and to engage them initially. But Timmons understood the gist.

"Thank you. Fatboy standing by. Out."

Timmons tossed the handset to the radioman in disgust.

"Wanker," he said. He ran back to the bridge and began watching the periscope.

While all this was going on in the radio shack, I had grabbed the ship's intercom and announced, "Fubars! General Quarters. Man your battle stations! Fubars, man your battle stations!" And I rang the ship's alarm. It didn't sound much like the Navy's General Quarters signal, but it was loud. Then I ran down the ladder to the main deck. Williams and Otto had uncovered the gun. The other four Fubars came running up and took their positions by the gun. Otto was searching for the U boat periscope. Williams was in the aiming chair cranking the elevation and bearing handles to lower and point the gun in the general direction of the threat. Reynolds removed the tompion that plugged and protected the muzzle of the gun and then jumped through the deck hatch into the temporary ammunition storage locker where we kept a dozen shells for just this sort of emergency. If we needed more, we'd have to go to the ship's magazine and manhandle some to the gun. There were no mechanical ammunition hoists on *Carlota*. Otto handed a shell up to Smithers who passed it to Pancho who cradled it and stood by for orders.

I was watching the periscope through my glasses. Being on the main deck we were about twenty feet lower than the pilot house, and it was hard to see. The truth was, I couldn't see anything. Maybe the U boat went down.

So we waited.

"Maybe he's one of ours," said Smithers.

"And maybe your dick will get longer," said Reynolds.

"It's long enough, asshole."

"That's what she said," said Reynolds.

"Straight up the middle, Jimmy."

There was no sense saying anything about this. It was just nerves. I wasn't feeling so chipper myself. We all knew the cargo we were carrying. A few nervous jokes were understandable under the circumstances.

We didn't have long to wait to get an answer. Just off the starboard beam, about three thousand yards away, a hideous black sea monster rose up from the smooth water, snout first followed by conning tower. It was pointing straight at us. I'm sure the German sailors on that U boat had some affection for their vessel, maybe even thought it had its finer points of aesthetics, but to us on the *Carlota* it was incongruous and as ugly as Grendel's mother, a hideous sea hag rising from a calm water, black and streaming white water as it slowly rose and leveled off. And through my glasses I could see crewmen coming up into the conning tower. I could even see the U boat skipper looking at us through his binoculars. All U boat skippers wore distinctive white hats. I couldn't see his face, but I could see that white officer's hat.

"That ain't one of ours," said Reynolds.

Williams saw it too, of course, and cranked both his aiming wheels to swing the gun on to the target. He was looking through the circular sight on the side of the gun as he worked the handles.

"There's your target, Williams," I said, unnecessarily. "Load!"

Pancho rammed a sleek three-inch shell into the breech and closed it.

"Got him, Williams?" I shouted.

"Yes, sir."

"Fire!"

An orange flame surrounded by a dark gray cloud of smoke shot from the muzzle. The noise was deafening and we all could feel the concussion of blast. The gun recoiled and the brass shell casing clattered and clanged on to the deck.

I watched to see the fall of shot. It must have passed well over the U boat, because I never saw the splash. The three-inch fifty is a flat shooting gun with a maximum range of more than six miles. Our shot could have passed just over the conning tower and still landed a mile beyond it.

"Over! Reload!" Pancho shoved anther round into the breech, and Williams cranked the elevation gear to lower the muzzle, still looking through the gunsight. I wondered how accurate that sight really was. It was like sighting in a telescopic lens on a rifle. If it wasn't lined up properly, you could point at a target all day, put the cross hairs right on him and yet never come close with your shot. I wondered who'd installed our gun and whether the sight was even remotely correct. A yardbird carelessly walking past and bumping the sight with a tool could throw the sight out of alignment and no one would ever know it. Even the slightest misalignment would mean inaccuracy. And the greater the range to the target, the greater the error. We had not been able to test fire the gun, so we had no idea whether it was at all accurate.

"Fire!"

Another miss, although I thought I saw the splash of the shot several hundred yards behind and to the right of the U boat. I wondered why the shell didn't explode. We were firing high explosives with contact fuses. They should have gone off when they hit the water. Maybe this one was a dud. Maybe there were some armor piercing shells mixed in. They had to hit something solid to go off. Armor piercing would have been just fine if we hit the U boat. It would go through the hull and do severe damage, but only if it hit metal. A close shot into the water wouldn't explode and would only soak the conning tower.

We kept firing—three, four more shots. I couldn't be sure of the fall of the shot. One shell hit the water and skipped off like a flat stone side-armed off the surface of a lake. Another hit the water and exploded.

Close but no cigar. Maybe we did some damage. You didn't have to hit a U boat to injure it. The shock waves from a nearby explosion could damage the pressure hull, maybe loosen a few plates or rivets—small injuries that could be fatal once the U boat submerged and the water pressure increased. Even an uninjured U boat could not go much below 300 feet. After that the water pressure would begin to crush the hull.

So maybe we were hurting him, but I couldn't see any real evidence of it.

Meanwhile the U boat was maneuvering for a shot. Normally they would sink a lonely, unarmed freighter with shells from their deck gun. But when they realized we had a gun ourselves, even though we weren't hitting them yet, they decided to use a torpedo. Probably they figured a merchant freighter like the *Carlota* was worth an expensive torpedo. The bean counters back at their admiralty wouldn't fuss about the expense. One torpedo would do the trick, if it hit us. Chances are they'd fire two, just to make sure. The Germans, just like the Americans, had trouble now and then with their torpedoes. They didn't always travel straight and they didn't always go off with they hit their target. Unless we could put a shell into their conning tower, a miss or a dud torpedo was our only hope.

Life was getting even more difficult because Timmons had ordered a violent full rudder turn to the right. I understood what he was doing. He was trying to point us head on to the U boat and give the Germans as small a target as possible, and maybe he was also trying to give the U boat captain a little scare by aiming *Carlota* for the sub, as if we were going to ram it. But the turning motion meant we couldn't get a steady aim on the U boat and the next two shots we fired went well wide, although the range was better. We might have hit if we could have had a steady platform to aim from, but Timmons had also ordered full speed ahead and *Carlota* was shuddering and shaking from the effort of turning at her maximum speed. Worse, as the ship swung around to face the U boat bows on, the gun became obstructed by the higher level of *Carlota*'s forecastle. And when we were headed straight on for the U boat we couldn't fire at all. We were like an old sail-driven man of war that could only really fire to the side, and as romantic as that might sound, it was no consolation for the fact that, although our maneuver may have reduced our silhouette as a target, it left us weaponless. So, the U boat would either miss with its torpedoes, or we'd had it. There was no way we could close the distance between us and ram the U boat. It was too far away and too nimble. It could fire and submerge before we got within a thousand yards.

I ran up the ladder to the forecastle deck and stood on the most forward part of the ship. I looked down on the creamy bow wave. There were no dolphins riding the wave just then. They were usually there in these waters, but not today. The poetically inclined would say the dolphins sensed our desperate predicament and wanted no part of it. In reality, they were just off somewhere doing something else.

I had my glasses focused on the U boat's conning tower. I could almost see the skipper's face. He was looking back at us through his aiming binoculars. I didn't know what they called them, but I understood what they did—they communicated the range and bearing of the target to the fire control system. We, of course, were the target.

Then I saw the skipper raise his hand and then lower it, as if ordering a cavalry charge. I thought it was unnecessary dramatics, but no sooner had he ordered fire than I saw a torpedo shoot into the air from just in front of the U boat. The torpedo rose like a fish after a fly. They're not supposed to do that, I thought. The torpedo cleared the water completely and then splashed back into the sea like a boy doing a belly flop. I couldn't see where it went after that. But that was a major malfunction and a piece of luck for *Carlota*.

Then I saw the second torpedo heading straight for us. I could see the wake caused by its propulsion gear. It was straight as a string. It seemed to be moving at the speed of light, although I knew its top speed was only around forty knots. That was plenty fast enough to handle *Carlota*. And we were helping things along by heading for it at our top speed, which wasn't very fast, but under the circumstances more than fast enough. As I watched the thing coming toward us, I had the absurd sensation that my shirt was too thin, as though the torpedo was aimed at me personally and was about to hit me squarely in the chest. I had felt that same sensation a time or two before, when someone was pointing a pistol at me. But this was no pistol. This was a lethal, blind missile, unattached and released from any human hand. It had nothing against me; it had nothing against any of us. That made it all the more frightful. There could be no negotiation. No defense.

At that moment Otto joined me at the bow.

"Son of a bitch!" he said. He could see the wake, too.

"Yes." I recalled a Sunday school lesson from Mr. Barnes, the village pharmacist. He told our class of ten-year-olds that if your last words were profane, you would take an immediate express elevator to hell. The girls ignored him because they didn't cuss, and the boys didn't pay attention, because last words and death were somebody else's problem. Even so, I thought of mentioning that to Otto, but I didn't.

We watched for what seemed like minutes, but were only a few seconds.

"Son of a bitch!" said Otto again.

Suddenly and unaccountably, the torpedo wake, which had been so noticeable moments ago, just disappeared.

"Where'd it go?" I said, not expecting any answer and gripping the railing hard, as though bracing for an explosion any second. And a fat lot of good my firm grip would have done, I thought.

"I dunno, sir," said Otto. "But it should have hit us by now."

"Another dud?"

"Could be."

"Is that possible?"

"Maybe. In sonar school they told us the Krauts were having trouble with the depth-keeping devices. Something's been messing them up. Maybe this one just took a dive. Either that or they set the depth too deep. *Carlota* doesn't draw as much as the normal freighter, so maybe they figured wrong. If they did, it went straight underneath us. It sure seemed like it was heading straight for us."

"Two malfunctions? What're the chances of that?"

"Not very good, sir. But we're still here."

On the conning tower of the U boat there was a sudden flurry of activity. Men were pointing to the sky to their right. We could hear the U boat's alarm horn go off. We could see the Germans hastily leaving the conning tower, their lookouts sliding down their ladders and disappearing below. The last to leave was the skipper in the white hat. And then we heard aircraft engines. *Ranger*'s combat air patrol?

Then we saw them. The first, a F4F Wildcat fighter, came swooping down out of the misting clouds, swooping like a beautiful wing-set raptor diving to snatch a fish from a stream or a mouse from a meadow. Swooping as he came on his strafing run, he opened fire, and we could see the puffs behind his wings as he fired fifty caliber machine gun rounds all around and into the U boat. Seemingly hundreds of splashes were thrown up, and for a moment almost obscured the U boat. I couldn't see if the conning tower was hit, but it was now deserted, and the U boat was starting to dive. But just behind the Wildcat came the slightly slower but even more deadly SBD Dauntless dive bomber. And he dropped from the clouds in a steeper dive than the Wildcat. I could see him twisting to the right in order to keep his bombing run on target with the fast submerging U boat. Down he came, and I wondered if the Germans on that U boat were having similar sensations to the ones I had just been feeling—not that they could *see* their doom coming. But they could imagine it. Then finally when it seemed the Dauntless pilot had waited too long and would crash into the sea, he pulled up and released two bombs that hit just about where the U Boat had gone under. We could feel the two explosions, the concussion and the blast, and the sea around the U boat erupted into two huge geysers—white with traces of aquamarine blue, beautiful beyond words, given the circumstances.

"Look at that!" yelled Otto. "Do you think they hit the bastard?"

"I don't know. But close enough is good enough. You know we only have to get within 300 yards or so with *Nameless*'s depth charges. So I figure it would be about the same with those bombs. I sure as hell hope so."

The two planes circled and both made strafing runs on the spot where the water was disturbed. Chances are the U boat had dived below a fifty caliber's reach. But maybe not.

I ran to the pilot house. Timmons was wide-eyed, but in control of himself. Captain Flynn was standing there in his bathrobe. He looked slightly stunned—bewildered by the fact that a stranger from another world had just appeared out of nowhere and tried to kill him. I could almost see him wondering, "What did I ever do to him?" And then two other strangers from another different world had suddenly appeared and come to the rescue. It was a hell of a way to wake up from a nap.

I heard the radio crackle.

"Fatboy-You-Idiot, this is Ghostrider, your friendly US cavalry, over."

I took the handset from the radioman.

"Ghostrider, this is Fatboy, just plain Fatboy, you boys arrived in the nick of time, over."

"Your tax dollars at work, Fatboy. Do you think we got him, over?"

"If not, he's going to need a change of underwear, over."

"We'll circle in case Fritz comes back, over."

"Roger, Ghostrider. We owe you a beer. A thousand thanks! You saved our ass, over."

"Roger, Fatboy. That's what we're here for. Ghostrider, out."

No one said anything for several minutes. Timmons had forgotten he'd ordered right full rudder and we were still turning. I didn't say anything about it. He'd notice sooner or later, and there were no contacts to worry about. Captain Flynn went back to his sea cabin to put on his pants. And I stood there looking out to the sea, the last traces of foam and white water were fading, and the sea was recovering its blue calm. All traces of the bombing were disappearing. Was it really over? It seemed so. At least for the time being.

But then Timmons pointed off to the left as we continued to turn right.

"My God! There he is again!"

The U boat was coming up again. That seemed strange. It didn't make sense. Why would he do that, with planes above? He had to believe that they'd be circling to make sure of their kill or to give it another try. If he wanted to take another shot at us, he could do it while submerged. What the hell was he doing?

There was definitely something different this time. The nose of the boat came jutting out of the water at about a forty-five degree angle. And stayed there. Almost the whole front section had come out slowly, but the conning tower remained submerged. That wasn't the way a submarine surfaced. Normally just the nose appeared but then the rest of the boat sort of bobbed to the surface and you saw the whole of its weather decks and superstructure almost at the same time. This was something different.

"I think he's been hit!" I said. "Damaged. He's trying to surface to save himself, but he's struggling."

The whole front section of the U boat was now out of the water, but at such an angle that we could see the bottom of the hull. We could see the deck gun, but the conning tower was still submerged, and we gradually understood that the boat was fighting a battle against flooding in his after section. The air pockets in his forward sections were struggling to keep him afloat. His engines and propellers were churning desperately to drive the boat upward against the pull of gravity and the weight of water. Probably the engine room was flooding, and soon the engines would quit, and the electrical systems would short out and the lights would go off and the men would be in utter darkness, and the only thing holding the boat up would be the air in the forward section. Their watertight doors would of course be closed and the sailors trapped in the flooding compartments would be in the process of drowning. But the men forward would be clinging to the bulkheads and valves and levers and pipes, as the U boat's nose slowly rose toward the vertical, and the men trapped inside held on, clutching anything they could grab on to. For a few seconds the air and water in the boat were in equilibrium, and the U boat hung there, engines straining. The Wildcat pilot saw what was happening and turned from his circling and made a strafing run on the U boat bow. He fired his fifty calibers and hits splashed all around what was now an ugly black obelisk. Then the pocket of air lost the fight against the weight of water, and the U boat started to sink, slowly at first, and then suddenly faster and faster still, and then the last of him slid down and disappeared in a boil of white water. And that was the end of the U boat and the seventy or so German sailors who, just a few minutes before, were trying to blow us and *Carlota* into nothingness. It was hard to feel sorry for those Germans, even though they were undergoing a terrifying and awful death, as their U boat collapsed in on them. They were crushed and drowned as they plunged a thousand feet or more to the bottom. I hoped they all died quickly, that their compartments collapsed and flooded all at once . . . hoped that there were no small air pockets left to offer a few extra minutes of terror. It was hard to feel too sorry. But some part of all of us felt it a little. No sailor likes to see a ship go down. It's too stark a reminder of things you don't want to think about.

CHAPTER SEVEN

THERE WERE NO SURVIVORS FROM THE U BOAT. THAT WAS NOT SURPRIS-ing, but we looked anyway in case one or two of them had managed to get out through their main hatch. Timmons had reduced speed to "ahead slow," and we circled and searched the surface for bobbing heads or men clinging to debris. But there was nothing. Just empty sea. Even the foam churned up by the U boat's plunge was rapidly fading, and the sea was returning to its usual indifference.

"Do you think we got him, Mister Fitzhugh?" said Otto. The Fubars were standing on the main deck alongside the gun as we scanned the surface for survivors.

"Well, we got some of him, I figure. At least, I think so. We shot. He sank. Who's to say who put the holes in him? We can't claim it all. But we *can* claim a partial. You bet."

"All right! Just like an assist in hockey, we get a point."

"He shoots! He scores!" said Otto.

"Straight up the middle, Jimmy," said Lefty.

"Good job, guys," I said. "Well done."

I meant it, too. The Fubars had done their job. Personally, I was pretty sure we didn't hit anything but the ocean. But there was no way to tell, and the men had behaved well and deserved credit for it. They'd like it if we could mark down a partial kill for our score, and it wouldn't mean anything one way or another to those Germans who were on their way to the bottom. Poor bastards.

Our search for survivors was hampered by the fact that we were still going in circles. Something must have gone wrong with the rudder. Either that or Timmons had forgotten to issue new orders. I went back up to the bridge where Timmons and Captain Flynn were conferring. The captain was still wearing his bathrobe, but he had put on his pants. He had no future as a male model.

"You know we're going in circles," I said.

"Yes, we've noticed," said Timmons gaily. "Bloody thing is stuck. I wonder if that second torpedo hit the rudder and jammed it. Didn't go off, thankfully, but maybe put a dent in it. Could be. That would be ironic, wouldn't you say? That's what happened to the *Bismarck*, which is how we were able to catch up with the old girl and sink her."

"Not a happy thought," I said.

"No, now that you mention it."

"I wonder if there's more of the bastards around," said Captain Flynn. "What do you think?"

"It's possible," I said. "But I kind of doubt it. The only report we have of wolf pack activity is in the Western Approaches to England. They hang around there where the convoys are coming in. No sense in sending multiple boats this far when the targets will come to them. Most of the U boat stuff off the Atlantic coast and in the Gulf of Mexico is lone wolves. Most likely this guy was on his own."

"Let's hope so," said Captain Flynn.

"What's the story with the rudder?" I said.

"We're working on it," said Captain Flynn. "It's not the rudder per se but rather the gearing that controls it. Just a little bit dicky for some reason. Nothing too serious, I hope. We'll be going nowhere, though—until we get it fixed."

"By that time the convoy could be out of reach," I said. "We can't steam fast enough to catch up to them, if they get too far ahead."

"Too true," said Flynn. "And I don't feature making this trip alone. I wonder if we should turn back."

I was afraid he was thinking that.

"We can't do that," I said. "We're carrying vital cargo."

"One more reason to think about turning back. Can you imagine what would have happened if that torpedo had hit? My old auntie in London would be short one nephew and one parrot."

I didn't say anything. We were not turning back under any circumstances. If I had to put the captain and all the crew over the side in lifeboats and run the ship myself with the Fubars, that's what we would do. We could do it, too, and I suspect the captain understood that.

"Maybe the convoy can slow down enough for us to catch up, once we get the steering gear fixed," I said. "We should send the flagship a message."

"All right. I suggest you write it. You know better than I do what the Navy boys like to hear. The snipes tell me they'll have us going straight again in roughly twelve hours." "Snipes" was the universal term for a ship's engineers.

Twelve hours. By that time it would certainly be too late to catch the convoy. They were already forty miles ahead. Another twelve hours steaming even at eight knots, while we sat motionless, meant almost another hundred miles. Even if we steamed at our maximum safe speed—safe in the sense that we wouldn't blow the metaphorical gasket and go dead in the water with no help in sight—at a prudent speed, in other words, we'd only be able to make up two miles every hour. That meant after waiting twelve hours, we'd be essentially three whole days behind. And the convoy would be making course changes as conditions and the tactical situation changed, so we might never be able to find them. We were only sure of the final destination—Casablanca. In fact, Captain Flynn had only learned where we were going after we cleared Norfolk harbor and he opened his sealed orders. But we couldn't be sure of the convoy's course to get there. Their course changes along the way would be designed to deceive any watchful enemy about the convoy's final destination. And those "watchful enemies"—either U boats or Luftwaffe—could pop up at any point in the voyage and therefore necessitate some tactical changes that were not part of the original plans. And the closer the convoy got to its target, the stricter the radio silence. We couldn't very well call up and ask where the hell they were. That was precisely the information they would not want to broadcast.

I looked out at the empty surface of the sea, as we slowly went around in circles, and thought that we were very alone, and likely to stay that way.

"Going around in circles," I said to myself. "Way too metaphorical."

I went down to my cabin to compose the message to the flagship. I would have to code it, before sending. I also wanted to be alone so I could take a deep breath after that close call with a torpedo. It was not just a message that needed composing.

I got out my code book and wrote the following: *Fatboy attacked by U boat. Damaged rudder. Estimate time to repair twelve hours. Please advise.*

The admiral would know from the pilots' report that they had got the U boat, and he would understand that I was asking for instructions about what to do next. I had a feeling what his response would be. I called the bridge and sent for the radio operator. He came, knocked on the door, and I gave him the coded message to send.

"Send this immediately and let me know as soon as you hear back."

"Okay," he said.

Okay? Well, you couldn't expect much from a civilian merchantman.

There was a pint of bourbon in my desk drawer, just like in the old days when I was a PI. All private detectives in LA were expected to have pints of bourbon in their desk drawers, right next to a spare thirty-eight. And when a beautiful and sultry client came in with a problem, you offered her a shot in a Dixie cup and waited for her to tell her story. That was the standard script, and any departure from the norm was considered bad form, like not owning a fedora. So this was like old home week, minus the sultry client. The bourbon was Rebel Yell, and I had bought it in Norfolk. It was cheap, but recognizable. I took it out and poured three fingers into my toothbrush glass, drank it down in two swallows and felt immediately better. Drinking on board a Navy ship is against the rules. But this was not a Navy ship. It was a civilian banana boat with a rusted bottom, a "dicky" steering gear, and a crew of jailbirds, not counting the Fubars. And we weren't going anywhere for a while. A generous shot of bourbon seemed justified. And if I was technically breaking the rules, I could live with it. I didn't worry about sharing with the Fubars. I was sure they had their own stash somewhere and would be discreet and professional while getting mildly drunk. For the moment there was really nothing for them to do, and they deserved a drink as much as I did. If another U boat showed its ugly head, we'd all be able to respond. I wasn't worried about that. The Fubars were all good men, even the ones who were still boys. And as I told Captain Flynn, I didn't think there was another Kraut around anywhere. If there was, I was pretty sure we wouldn't get lucky a second time anyway, so what the hell difference did it make if we blew up with Rebel Yell on our breath?

The *Carlota* wasn't much of a vessel when viewed from most angles, but she did have the advantage of civilian furniture and fixtures. Unlike the *Nameless* and every other Navy ship, *Carlota* had colors in her spaces. Navy ships were relentlessly gray inside and out. The sea was usually blue, but it had its gray moods too, as did the sky, and it was only when you finally got back to shore and looked around that you realized how starved for color you had been. You felt like you were in the *Wizard of Oz*, when the movie goes from black and white to technicolor. So it was kind of pleasant to sit in my cabin on the *Carlota*, with its flowery, sarong-like upholstery. It was faded, maybe, and musty smelling, but still a nice, cheery change from gray. And thinking of sarongs got me thinking about Dorothy Lamour in those South Sea island movies she made, and that naturally got me wondering what she'd look like if someone unwrapped her from that piece of flowered silk. I had met her at a party once in Hollywood, and it was a question that was definitely worth pondering. I pondered it at the time, and I pondered it now. That night at the party she had a pleasant smile that I interpreted as encouraging. I asked her if she was seeing anyone at the moment, and she said she was, "but things do change." Then she flashed an even more encouraging smile and sashayed away. She didn't look back over her shoulder and wink, but I figured she thought about it. As an actress she was only passable, but she knew how to exit a scene, leaving them wanting more. Thinking of Dorothy without her sarong then got me thinking about Martha—not that there was much similarity between the two. Martha was slim and blonde; Dorothy, curvaceous and dark. But I had the advantage of actually knowing how Martha looked without a sarong, or without anything else, for that matter. I remembered being with her on that beach on the south coast of Cuba, and I remembered the two of us together in the sleeping bag and the way the stars looked and sound of the surf and all the rest of what happened that night. And I remembered how she sang softly, almost in a whisper, "*What'll I do when you are far away and I am blue, what'll I do.*"

She wasn't much of a singer, but she was a hell of a whisperer. Well—"son of a bitch," I said out loud. Best not to think too hard about any of that. I knew I was having a typical sailor's reaction to being at sea. Well, what of it? It was only natural. You spend enough time at sea, and you'll have impure thoughts about everyone from Betty Grable to Ma Joad, as well as anyone waiting for you at home. It didn't matter whether they actually *were* waiting, or whether they even *knew* they were supposed to be waiting. And it didn't matter whether you really cared that they *had* waited, once you got back. Sailors are Pygmalions who can make a Galatea out of a cross-eyed girl from first period algebra, and she'll get more and more beautiful as the weeks go by, up until it's time to go back home and confront reality. And more often than not, having looked reality in the face, and listened to it, sailors are ready to go back to sea and start all over again. It's an unwritten law that sailors need their romantic imaginations to be well oiled and fully functioning. Otherwise they think too much and in their mind's eyes see images of Grendel's mother rising black and evil from the bottomless ocean.

I guess I was also having some sort of delayed reaction to that U boat attack—replacing some terrible and frightening images with pictures of smiling women. Well, then, so be it, and thank you, Martha, and thank you, Dorothy, and, what the hell, thanks to you too, Ma Joad. Welcome, ladies, to my mind's eye and my imagination. Come on in and sit down and make yourselves comfortable. Tell Grendel's mother to get lost, and feel free to take off those sarongs.

CHAPTER EIGHT

A FEW MINUTES LATER THE RADIOMAN RETURNED WITH A MESSAGE from the flagship. I sat down and decoded it.

Proceed independently. Arrive 1200 Position Ilsa D Day Minus One. Good luck.

I figured. In other words, head for the Casablanca rendezvous by yourself and be there, noon sharp, on the day the invasion convoy arrives. Ah, yes. Nothing to it.

Position Ilsa was the code name for a spot one hundred miles or so off the coast of Casablanca. The plan was for the convoy, at that point, to split into three separate attack groups. One would head south to land at Safi, which was down the coast from Casablanca by a good fifty miles. The center would attack Casablanca more directly by landing at Fedhala, a smaller port on the northern suburbs of the city. And the northern group would land at the mouth of the Sebou River, fifty miles above Casablanca. *Carlota* was assigned to the northern group. Somewhere off the mouth of the Sebou, Rene would meet us and guide us up the river to the French airbase at Port Lyautey. So the task ahead was simple enough to understand. It was quite a bit more difficult to achieve. There were thousands of miles of ocean ahead of us and getting there on time would be tricky, to say the least. If we didn't get there, the attack up the Sebou would be jeopardized, and I wondered, not for the first time, whether there was a Plan B. Bunny had suggested that there was, but he didn't bother to tell me what it was. Well, that was not surprising. And it wasn't from carelessness, either. Everyone in this business operated on a need-to-know basis, and it was assumed that I only needed to know Plan A. If it failed, then the generals would make adjustments and move on. The *Carlota* would become a mere footnote in the history of the campaign. If that. In other words, *Carlota's* mission was important, but if she blew up on the way to Casablanca, it would be too bad, but something else would take her place and our disappearance from the picture would not be a disaster to anyone other than the relatives of the crew and the owner of the ship. Or his insurance company. As for myself, I had no real relatives to worry about. The gang of broken-down writers at the Garden of Allah Hotel would shed a maudlin tear or two. And raise their glasses. And Hobey would write a treatment for a movie about me, submit it, and have it rejected. And that would be that. The idea made me smile, because like most men going into harm's way, I could imagine the worst without really believing it would happen. The ones who sincerely did believe it were not much use. Horrifying images of personal catastrophe immobilized them. My sometime friend—and Martha's husband—Ernest Hemingway said something about cowardice being almost always the inability to stop the imagination, or something like that. Maybe. But it seemed to me that it was more about not being able to imagine anything else—anything other than personal disaster. Man has only so much room in his imagination, so if you keep it stocked with images that look good on the wall or in a frame, like Captain Flynn's Beatrice, you stand a better chance of not imagining things that put you out of action. Maybe that's what Hemingway meant. The next time I see him, maybe I'll ask him what he thinks of that. On second thought, maybe not. As Bunny always says, it's best not to get too friendly with the husbands.

The overall strategy for the Moroccan operation called for the three attack groups to be in their positions by midnight of D Minus One. The troop transports would anchor roughly eight miles from the beaches and lower their boats. Then they'd begin loading the troops, tanks, artillery, and supplies into the assault boats. Loading would take four hours, which meant the three-pronged assault could begin at 0400, Day D. The assault boats would then all assemble at the "point of departure," which was roughly two miles from shore; they would hit the beaches before the sun rose. This would happen at all three invasion points more or less simultaneously. Everyone was hoping that the element of surprise could be maintained, and that it would reduce the chances of French resistance. Surprise, confusion, inertia, and muddled politics would work together to convince the French to shrug and welcome us for morning coffee and croissants. With that hope in mind, and not wishing to kill anyone without having to, and not wishing to destroy buildings, bridges, or railway lines unnecessarily, there would be no naval bombardment and no aerial bombing of the three landing points. The Allies didn't know much about amphibious assaults at this point in the war, but they did know that things were likely to go better if they bombed and blasted the enemy's defenses *before* sending the assault troops ashore. The British debacle at Dieppe had proved that much, although it shouldn't have cost the English and Canadians three thousand dead to learn it. A ten-year-old boy could have figured that out for them. But because of the tangled French political questions, there'd be no bombardment this time—not unless and until the French decided to fight. We would not fire unless fired upon. And if our guys felt a little put upon by that decision, they had every reason. Somebody once said that democracy was three wolves and a lamb voting on what to have for lunch. Maybe. Maybe not. But military planning sometimes seemed like four blind men drawing up the map for a bicycle race. Sometimes there was no choice, because the information you needed was incomplete or not even available. That was bad enough. But in this case you had to think the French, who were supposed to be our Allies—and had been until they collapsed—might have given us a clue about their intentions, one way or the other. Maybe they had. But it certainly didn't seem like it. All of our planning was based on the fact that things could go either way.

Now that I knew where we were supposed to go and that we were on our own, the calculations were pretty simple. Part of the convoy had left yesterday, and the rest this morning. It was October 24th. We had been the last to leave and were about forty miles behind when the U boat attacked. Our dicky rudder meant we would not be able to start again until that night. To be on the safe side, we should probably figure on starting the next day—on the morning of the 25th. D Day in Morocco was scheduled for November 8th, so we were supposed to arrive at the

Point Ilsa rendezvous at noon on the 7th. That gave us fourteen days. If we steamed at a steady twelve knots, we would conserve fuel and not tax the engines and still be able to make a little over 4,000 miles in that time. Allowing for delays from bad weather and for currents that required regular course corrections and occasional minor engine problems of who-knew-what-kind, it was just possible that we could do it. There was no way to figure on troubles from U boats or long-range Luftwaffe bombers. If they showed up, we'd be lucky to avoid Doomsday, and we'd be grateful to arrive anywhere, at any time, much less at Position Ilsa.

Yes, it was just possible that we could do it. It was equally possible that we didn't have a prayer.

Mulling over the two possibilities, I realized that the odds of success were against us. Failure was staring us in the face and grinning. Well, I thought, it couldn't be helped. And besides, I wasn't a career Navy officer; I was only in the Navy for the duration of the war. I had no professional future, no grand illusions or ambitions to be ruined. When it was all over, I intended to go back to civilian life in Hollywood and see if Dorothy Lamour was still smiling. And if she wasn't, then someone else would be. That was the one thing in that town that you could be sure of. Not that I was forgetting Martha, mind you, but after all, she was married and therefore not dependable. Well, I told myself, all we could do was our best, and the results would be what they were. It was cold comfort, but there wasn't any warm comfort on the menu.

I went back up to the bridge to confer with Captain Flynn and Timmons and to draw a straight line on the chart between Norfolk and Casablanca. Due east.

Flynn and Timmons were both there. Flynn had put on a dark wool shirt. He wore his skipper's hat and looked vastly better and more salty than he did as Tweedledee in a bathrobe.

"What does the Admiral have to say for himself?" said Flynn.

"He congratulates you and the crew of the *Carlota* on the success of your battle with the U boat."

"Really? He said that?"

"Yes." It was a lie, but I figured it was a harmless one, if there is such a thing. And there is, of course.

"Well, that's very decent of him, I must say," said Captain Flynn. "Personally, I can't take too much credit, since during most of the action, I was in the head, throwing up. A touch of *mal de mer*. It comes on at the most inconvenient times. But still, it *was* a famous victory."

"Yes, sir," said Timmons, "And as someone once said, 'Victory has many fathers, defeat is an orphan.' So we all can take some pride in it. And there may even be some recognition from the high and mighty for us all."

"True," said Flynn. "And as one of this victory's several fathers, I shall be more than satisfied with a peerage as my reward."

"I think it only fair," said Timmons.

"As my title, I shall select 'Lord Boomerang of the Outback.' Has a nice ring to it. What do you say, Timmons?"

"Yes, sir. And since we are still obliged to go in circles, it is a particularly appropriate title. For myself, I would be happy to make the Honors List in any capacity, although a knighthood would be especially nice. *Honi Soit Qui Mal Y Pence*."

"What's that mean?" I said.

"It's the motto of the Knights of the Garter. Roughly translated, it means, '*If you don't like it, that's too fucking bad*.'"

"I'm surprised the English knights have a French motto," I said.

"I am, too, now that you mention it. I suppose it sounds fancier that way. Some might say the English version is rude. Well, did the admiral have any orders for us? Perhaps like 'Return to Norfolk and take the rest of the war off'?"

"There were orders, yes. He said—don't worry about catching up with the convoy. Just go along by yourselves and arrive at the assigned rendez-vous precisely fourteen days from now, at precisely high noon."

"Hmm. Is that all? Did he say anything else?"

"Yes. *Honi soit qui mal y pense*."

"Interesting that the admiral speaks French."

"That probably came from General Patton. He's in command of the Army side of things. He's a very cultured man."

"Drinks wine and so on?" said Timmons.

"Yes."

"I've heard of him," said Flynn. "Said to be something of a stormy petrel."

"That, too," I said.

"I'll bet he leapt at the chance to lead this attack."

"Actually, the way I heard it, he didn't want anything to do with it, at first. Said it was an impossible project and would end in disaster. It was only when FDR said 'Well then, OK, we'll find some other general to command' that Patton changed his mind and became enthusiastic."

"All disasters are equal, but some are . . ." Timmons paused. "What's the line I'm looking for?"

"I dunno," I said. "But I do know that we don't have any time to waste, so how's the rudder coming along?"

Captain Flynn shrugged resignedly.

"We should have it fixed in time to get underway tonight."

"Good. That'll give us a few extra hours I hadn't counted on. But there is some good news. Since there are three of us, we can divide the underway watches—four on, eight off. That'll make the trip a little more comfortable." I had been expecting to be on the bridge almost constantly, if we were sailing in convoy. I figured station keeping would be a continuing problem. And the captain and first mate would have been standing "port and starboard" watches—four hours on, four off. Sailing independently would be much easier on all of us. "That's assuming you trust me to stand watch on your ship, Captain."

"Oh, of course. We're under the Navy's orders, anyway. Glad to have you."

A merchant ship usually sails with a minimal crew. In part, that's a way to keep expenses down, since after all they are commercial ventures. It's also because, unlike a Navy ship in which the crew is constantly working to maintain the ship in perfect condition, a merchant vessel doesn't worry too much about anything except keeping the power plant going. Any maintenance to the hull and superstructure can be done periodically in port by local shipyards. And that sort of thing can be, and often is, put off until the last possible minute, when the ship is about to sink, from age or neglect. That's why some merchantmen are called "tramp steamers" and sail the seas looking like a shabby old lady pushing a shopping cart and muttering about her cats. Underway, there's usually only a helmsman and a ship's officer on the bridge, and that's about it. The officer is responsible for navigational changes, taking the ship's position regularly and making sure it's on course. The helmsman just steers the ordered course and waits for the officer to order any course changes or to make any maneuvers in case of traffic or imminent collisions or navigational hazards. As a result, most merchant officers are highly skilled seamen. There's very little specialization. They need to know pretty much everything about operating a ship at sea. And they do things with a stripped-down crew. But most of them don't seem to care about the condition of the ship. Or if they do, they know there's very little they can do about it.

"Well, gentlemen," said Timmons, "we're on the road to Morocco. Just like the film. Have you seen it? It just came out."

"No. But I know someone in Hollywood who worked on the script."

"Really? The very first scene shows a ship blowing up, and then you see Hope and Crosby floating on a raft. I hope that's not an omen. Later they meet an Arab princess played by Dorothy Lamour."

"She has nice lips," said the captain. "Very full. My aunt would have no trouble reading her."

"Speaking of that," said Timmons, "I wonder what the women will be like in Casablanca. Do all the Arab women wear veils, or just the homely ones?"

"How do you know the ones wearing veils are homely?" I said.

"Ha, ha! Good question. It's an empirical problem. What was Bishop Berkeley's famous wheeze? *Esse est percepi*—'To be is to be perceived.' Yes, that was it. So, if you accept that proposition—if you believe that *to be is* bloody well *to be perceived*—does beauty actually exist, if you can't perceive it?" Timmons smiled in an abstracted sort of way, as though admiring the light bulb that had gone off above his head. "Wouldn't that old sod, Dr. Grimes, be surprised to hear us discussing British empiricism? He thought I was not paying attention all those years. Ha! That's one in his eye."

"Here's another one for you—if a parrot doesn't talk, does it mean he has nothing to say?" said Captain Flynn.

"Yes. Another philosophical question!" said Timmons. "Although I don't see how it fits with Berkeley. But perhaps it does, somehow."

"And if all the Arab women wear veils," said the captain, "my aunt would not be able to understand any of them, beautiful or otherwise. She would know *that* they were talking by the puffing out of the veil from their breath, but she could not know *what* they were saying. Then, she might well ask herself, were they actually saying anything or merely breathing heavily?"

"Yes. I suppose she would," said Timmons. He seemed a little puzzled, though, by the captain's interest in deaf aunts and parrots.

I had listened to more than a few idiotic conversations like this. Watches at sea are generally uneventful, and sailors do sometimes talk about things other than women and favorite bars. So this was not new. And that was, I thought, a good thing. I was glad, or rather relieved, that the captain and Timmons were apparently in pretty fair spirits. Flynn had recovered from his bout of "*mal de mer.*" Or possibly "*mal de U boat.*" Like Timmons, I couldn't see how the captain's parrot comments made much sense. It all seemed a little odd, but then Flynn seemed a little odd even before the U boat attack, so I could hope that this latest outbreak was nothing more than his usual eccentricity and not some sort of delayed hysteria. We had a long trip in front of us, long in more ways than one, and we would need all our reserves of concentration and good feeling. We all seemed pretty well resigned to the task ahead. And the only sour note seemed to be the helmsman, who was looking disturbed about something and was moving his lips as though talking to himself. He was the same swarthy Mediterranean I had noticed before. I wondered if he was part of the regular crew or one of the Norfolk jailbirds.

"What's that fellow's name?" I said to Timmons. "The helmsman."

"Him? Oh, he's one of the new boys. I think he goes by Ali. Or Achmed. Something like that. Maybe he can explain about the veils."

"You're letting a new boy at the helm?"

"His papers were in order. Rated Able-Body Seaman. Had a good reference. And we're desperately shorthanded, you know."

"Yes. I know."

"But of course we'll keep an eye on him to make sure he's up to scratch."

"Of course."

CHAPTER NINE

I PASSED THE WORD OVER THE SHIP'S INTERCOM FOR WILLIAMS TO come to the bridge. He showed up in a minute or two.

"Yes, sir?"

"I need to have a word with the Fubars. Get them together and come to my cabin in fifteen minutes. OK?"

"Aye, aye, sir."

Fifteen minutes later, on the dot, there was a knock on my cabin door.

"Come on in, guys. Make yourselves comfortable." They sat down on the rattan couch and chairs. I perched on the desk. "First of all, I have a confession to make to you," I said. "I did not spend the last few weeks in bed with the Andrews Sisters."

"We never thought you did, sir," said Reynolds. "We give you more credit than that."

"Thank you, Reynolds. Your confidence in me is a great comfort in times of trouble. No, I was really on a special assignment for the OSS, which is the Office of Strategic Services. Basically one of our intelligence agencies."

"Spies?" said Lefty.

"Yes. I was in Casablanca on a mission."

They nodded and smiled. They approved.

"Do the women all wear veils?" said Reynolds.

"Only the ugly ones. It's a very old civilization, and they have thought these things through. But the point is, I learned a little bit about what's going on there, and that is relevant, because when we get the god-damn rudder straightened out, that's where we're going. We're taking this bucket to meet the convoy off the coast of Morocco. We're part

77

of Operation Torch, which is going to land 35,000 troops in Morocco, take Casablanca and, ultimately, the whole country. Another Allied force is coming down from England, and they'll sail through the Straits of Gibraltar into the Med and land in two places in Algeria. Everything is timed to go off simultaneously. Not an easy thing to do. We would have gone with the convoy, but we got a late start, and this business with the U boat set us back a day. We just got orders to proceed independently. Since we wouldn't be able to catch up with them now, we'll meet them there."

They looked at each other. They knew what that meant. Or what it could mean.

"So the next question is—what about the *Carlota*? I'm not worried about *Carlota*'s captain and first mate. They seem professional, and they're on board with the mission. But I'm not so sure about the crew. You may know this, but *Carlota*'s regular crew scattered when they heard rumors about where we might be going and what we definitely were carrying. The cargo alone was enough to send them running."

"Pussies," said Otto.

"The Navy was, and is, shorthanded, so they emptied the Norfolk jail and gave us the scrapings. And they may have scooped up some other characters hanging around the docks. I'm sure you've noticed that most of these birds are not Americans, and there's at least one who's some kind of Arab."

"That's Ali, sir," said Smithers. "He showed me a picture of his wife."

"Was she wearing a veil?" said Pancho.

"Yes."

"Poor guy. Course he ain't nothing to look at either, so maybe it's fair."

"Well," I said, "we don't really care about his love life. What we care about is getting this tub to Morocco on time and in good shape. So I want you guys to keep an eye on Ali, and I want you to find out if there are any other Arabs in the crew—friends of his. Here's why that might matter. Morocco is essentially a French colony. They call it a protectorate, but that's like calling Stalin 'the people's choice.' Nobody invited the French in there. The population of the country is overwhelmingly Arab. Most of them don't like the French and don't like the fact that they are there, even though they've made the trains run on time and built the cities into livable places that Europeans like. Sidewalk cafes and what have you. But most Arabs would just as soon do without all that stuff, and a lot of them would like to kick the French out. Plus the fact that the French treat the Arabs like second-class citizens, and the Arabs resent it. The same is true in Algeria, which is just next door. Twenty years or so ago the Arabs fought a bloody war against the French, and they're still not happy about losing."

"Like in Beau Geste," said Otto.

"Right. That's the main reason there's a heavy French military presence in Morocco and Algeria—to keep the lid on the local Arabs."

"The Foreign Legion's there?"

"Yep. As well as some regular Army and Navy—and Air Force. So that's the picture—for the last twenty years unhappy Arabs have been sitting around drinking coffee and wondering how in the hell they can get rid of these frog-eating foreigners. Then along comes World War Two, and that gives them an idea."

"Team up with the Krauts."

"Right. So . . . a lot of Arabs are secretly on the side of the Germans and hoping that they win and kick the French out of Algeria and Morocco. The Krauts are already in North Africa—in Tunisia, and they are currently knocking the crap out of our British friends in Egypt. And the last thing the Krauts want is for the Yanks and the Brits to sneak through the back door into western North Africa. So they've recruited a lot of Arabs to work behind the scenes to keep them posted on what the French are up to. And what we're up to, if possible. And they're also training them for potential sabotage missions. The Krauts don't know for sure that we're planning to invade Morocco and Algeria—at least that's what we're hoping. But they have to know it's a possibility, since everyone has been yelling about a second front, and the Krauts have to know that North Africa is one possible target."

"Don't these Arabs realize that if the Germans win, they'll stay there, and they'll be a lot worse than the French?"

"As a Hollywood producer once said, they'll jump off that bridge when they come to it. First things first."

TERRY MORT

"So you figure Ali might be one of them? That he's working for the Krauts?"

"I think it's a possibility we can't afford to overlook. The big brass have put out the word that this convoy is a routine troop transport to England. That was for the benefit of any German agents who were watching—and we have to operate on the assumption there are some. It would be naïve not to. But—no agent worth his knockwurst is going to believe that this is a routine convoy, because no routine convoy also consists of transports crammed with troops, battleships, attack aircraft carriers, cruisers, and a couple dozen destroyers. It's obviously an offensive operation—which is why there were those rumors that scared off the *Carlota*'s regular crew. So—let's assume the agents are watching the loading. They see what's going into *Carlota*'s belly."

"We're a floating bomb."

"Right. All it would take is for somebody to throw a lighted Lucky Strike into the hold, and that would be the sad end of the *Carlota*. The blast and fire from *Carlota* would do quite a bit of damage to the others in the vicinity. The ships in convoy would be only one thousand yards apart. It would be setting off a huge bomb in the middle of the convoy."

"But let's say Ali or someone else throws the lighted Lucky, he'll blow himself up with the rest of us."

"Maybe. Maybe he wants to be a martyr. Maybe his wife really needs that veil and he's tired of living. But maybe not. Maybe he's planning to steal a lifeboat first and get out before a fire causes an explosion. Maybe he's got some kind of explosive device that could be fused to allow him time to get away before it goes off. Maybe he's got a partner who'll help launch the lifeboat."

"And if he got picked up by one of the other ships he could say anything about how he escaped. No one would be around to say otherwise."

"That's right. I know this cloak and dagger stuff may sound a little farfetched, but during my time in the OSS I learned that sabotage is going to be a big part of this war. Both sides are thinking of things like this and trying to do them. I should say—are doing them."

"Yes, sir, but what was Ali doing in the Norfolk jail?"

"I don't know. But I do know it's not hard for a sailor to get arrested in Norfolk. And as I said, maybe he wasn't in jail at all. Maybe he just joined the crew at the last minute and said he was one of the jailbirds. It wouldn't be hard for a German agent to recruit a guy like him, especially if Ali was just hanging around the dockyards. And anyone who thinks there aren't Nazi agents working in the US has got his head up his ass. My buddies in the FBI tell me they've already picked up eight of them—four in New York and four in Florida. Both gangs were dropped off by U boats. And what better place to have an agent lurking around than Norfolk? It would be easy enough supply a guy like Ali with the makings for a bomb. Lots more efficient than a lighted cigarette. And it wouldn't have to be very big."

"No, it wouldn't," said Williams, seriously. "A small package of plastic explosive, something that could fit in your pocket, would be enough to ignite the Av gas. A pencil fuse would give him time to get off the ship before detonation—end of story."

"But none of those Nazi agents could have known that we were going to have problems and have to sail by ourselves."

"No. That's true. But as I said, my guess is they were hoping *Carlota's* explosion would damage some of the convoy too. I know this secret agent stuff may sound like Hollywood bullshit, but maybe you'll believe me when I tell you that the OSS boys in Morocco are working on all kinds of dirty tricks. They're developing plastic explosives that look like mule turds, so that if the Krauts ever invade Morocco and their trucks run over this stuff, the shit will hit the fan, literally. And the OSS even dressed up some anonymous dead guy in an officer's uniform and dumped him off the coast of Spain with phony ID and phony invasion plans in his pocket. The idea is that the plans will get to Franco and Franco'll send them to his pal Hitler, and Hitler will wet his pants and send an army to Fuckyouistan or someplace to repel an invasion that isn't coming. And all this kind of stuff—booby traps, saboteurs behind the lines, spies and double agents, phony information—all of it is going on in Morocco and Algeria and all through Europe, for that matter, and it's only going to get worse as the war gets nastier."

"Where's Fuckyouistan, Boss?"

"That's classified," I said.

"But there's something I don't understand, sir. That U boat that attacked us—why would he do that if they had an agent on board?"

"You're assuming the U boat skipper knew about this plan. Most likely he didn't. But even if he did, you know the old expression, a bush in the hand is worth any number of birds. A skipper gets rewarded for sinking ships. Do you think he'd give a damn about some anonymous Arab deck hand, if he had a chance to score on a freighter?"

"No, sir. I guess not."

"Besides, we were sailing alone. If the U boat skipper did know of the sabotage plan, he'd expect us to be with the convoy."

"I still can't believe he missed," said Otto.

"Me either, frankly," I said. "But it may have been because we have such a shallow draft. That's important, because we—meaning you and me and this ship—have a very specific and important role in this invasion. We're not just hauling cargo. When we get there we're going to go up a shallow Moroccan river and knock off a French garrison and take their airfield."

"The Fubars?"

"Not quite. We're going to take a bunch of Army Special Ops guys. We'll pick them up when we rendezvous with the fleet."

"I don't get it. I thought the French lost the war to the Germans. How come they're still running things in their colonies?"

"It was part of the so-called Armistice agreement with the Krauts. As long as the French play ball, the Krauts would rather let them administer the colonies. Less work and less trouble for the Germans. But I know for a fact that the Gestapo are thick as fleas in Morocco and Algeria, and if the French don't play along, the Germans might just say the hell with it and take over—not just the colonies, but the rest of France. Right now they're only occupying the upper half and letting the collaborationists run the other half from the new capital in Vichy."

"I thought the French were on our side."

"Some of them are; others might be, if things fall right. In that case, when we land in Morocco, there'll be no fighting. But they might not be, in which case there'll be a battle."

"What's wrong with those guys?"

"I can't answer that one, Lefty. And neither can anyone else. Let's just say they can't agree among themselves on anything. Some will want to fight because they're loyal to the Vichy government, which is somehow willing to go along with Hitler; some will want to welcome us with open arms. Some will wait to see how things are going and then throw in with the winners. Some are worried that if they don't resist us, Hitler will blow his stack and occupy the whole of France as well as the colonies. That would put the Vichy government out of business. Some will do nothing, so that afterward, at some future day of reckoning, they can claim they were part of the resistance to the Germans, and the fact that no one knew about it just goes to show how good they were at secret warfare and espionage. French politics—especially after the surrender—are impossible to figure out, and it's just as impossible to predict what these bastards in Morocco will do. Even their General DeGaulle moans about the impossibility of governing a country that has two hundred forty-two different kinds of cheese. So we have to prepare for the worst case."

"Meaning we have to assume they're going to fight."

"Right. And we're carrying stuff our troops and pilots will need when they get there. So of all the ships in the invasion convoy, we're one of the most important. Of course, any potential Arab agent would not know any of that, but any crewman on this ship knows what we're carrying."

"If we're so all-fired important, why the hell didn't the convoy wait for us to get our rudder squared away?"

"Good question. The fact is, this is a huge operation, and the timing is very tight. They couldn't afford to wait without throwing the whole plan off schedule. As I said, there's a second big fleet coming down from England, too. The truth is, if we don't make it for some reason or other, there's a backup plan. But we're definitely Plan A, and so we're going to do everything we can to make sure we get it done."

"So what do you want us to do, sir?" said Williams.

"First of all keep an eye on the crew—and especially Ali. Be friendly with him, if you can, but don't bring up anything I said about politics. As far as anyone in the civilian crew knows, you guys know nothing. You don't know where we're going, and you never heard of Casablanca. If Ali

or any of his buddies say something suspicious or act kind of funny or
odd, let me know about it. See if he has anyone else close to him, especially another Arab. Or maybe some guy from central Europe. A lot of
them are in bed with the Krauts. I'll ask the captain to muster the crew
for some reason, so I can get a look at them. But you keep your eyes open,
too. Second, I've changed my mind about the watches. We're going to set
a regular two-man watch on the main deck, round the clock. Both men
will keep on the move and constantly surveil three primary areas—the
hatches to the hold, the life boats, and the gun and ammunition locker.
All the holds are shut tight now and secured. Lower deck doors to the
hold are locked from the inside, so that the only way in is through the
main deck hatches. We need to make sure no one is hanging around
those hatches. There are six of you, so four hours on, eight off. Nothing
that you're not used to. We'll be traveling darkened ship, which means the
watch standers at night will have to be especially alert. Anything moving
or scuttling around in the shadows better have four legs and whiskers. I'll
be standing regular underway watches on the bridge, but I expect to be
up there for more than just my watch, so I'll be another pair of eyes on
the main deck, at least part of the time. Third, wear your side arms at all
times, loaded, whether on watch or off. On watch, you will also carry a
twelve gauge. If anyone threatens you or the safety of the ship or tries to
break into the hold or the ammunition locker, shoot him."

"Shoot first and ask questions later?"

"Otto, you know as well as I do that a man shot with a twelve gauge
or a forty five is not going to have much to say afterward."

"What if we make a mistake?"

"Try not to. But if you do, I'll write to the widow."

"You sound serious, Boss."

"I am. And so is the Navy. I have orders to take command of the ship,
if I think it's necessary—for any reason. That's why they sent me here.
And I asked for you guys, because I know I can depend on you." That
was nothing but the truth, and the men knew it. "For the next two weeks
we'll be riding in a floating bomb. We're not going to take any chances.
There's a blonde I'd like to see again."

"None of the Andrews Sisters are blonde," said Reynolds.

"I know. And I think we've worn that joke out, Reynolds. Think of something new."

"Aye, aye, sir."

"You guys have any booze left?"

"A little."

"Save it. No drinking from here on out—unless and until I give the word. When we pull this off, I'll throw a party for us in Casablanca. Champagne and dancing girls. Till then, don't even smell the cork."

"Will the dancing girls be wearing veils, sir?"

"Yes, but nothing else."

"Will your blonde be there, sir?"

"I doubt it, but you never know."

That was true enough. With Martha, you never did know where she'd turn up. But I knew where she'd want to be, and where she'd try her damnedest to be—wherever the action was. And we were definitely headed for the action—the biggest operation of the war, so far.

"Any other questions?"

"Who's the blonde, sir?"

"Kate Smith. Anything else? OK. That's all. Main deck watches start immediately. Get together and figure out the schedule among yourselves. Three sections, two men each."

They left, and as I shut the door I could hear Smithers say to Reynolds—"I think Fitzy is bullshitting us again."

Yeah?" said Reynolds. "How?"

"Kate Smith ain't a blonde."

"Nothing gets by you, does it, Smitty."

Chapter Ten

A half an hour later I went up to the bridge. Captain Flynn had the watch. The helmsman was a burly blond giant with a happy expression. His name was Patkul.

"He's a Lett," said Captain Flynn. "He's been with me for a number of years now. Didn't run away when most of the others did. The Letts are a Baltic people, you know. Right, Patkul?"

"Yes, Captain." He grinned. He seemed friendly and content with his role in life.

"I always think of Cole Porter when I think of the Baltic people, don't you?" said Flynn to me.

"Cole Porter? Not really."

"You know the line—*'Lithuanians and Letts do it, Let's do it, Let's fall in love.'* Porter was very clever with his lyrics. Fond of puns. Good lyrics stick in your mind."

That was true. Whenever I thought of Martha, I thought of the line, "What'll I do when you are far away." Cole Porter didn't write that one. It was Irving Berlin. But I understood the broader point.

"And whenever I go into a house of ill fame, also known as a cat house," said the captain, "I think of his tune, Love For Sale. *'Old love, new love, every love but true love.'*"

Captain Flynn's singing was very bad.

"When you think of it," he said, "that's an example of the way words can have different meanings to different people. Or at different times or different contexts. That causes many of the world's problems, of course. Misunderstanding. That thought is not original with me, by the way. But take for example the word love—if it had only one single meaning that everyone understood and agreed upon, then the expression 'true love' would be a tautology, wouldn't it? Like saying the 'honest truth.' Or 'widow woman.' And 'false love' would be an oxymoron. But no. Love can mean many things, including the exchange of sex for money. Which is as far from the other definition as you can get, it seems to me. Don't get me wrong. I don't look down my nose at bordellos. I have made a small study of them over the years. Or perhaps I should say a medium-sized study. I don't make use of them more than is absolutely necessary, though, because I sometimes feel that would mean being unfaithful to Beatrice. But then I ask myself—would it be? After all, Beatrice wouldn't know anything about it, so did it actually happen from her point of view? It goes back to the question of veils and the philosophical Berkeley—'To be is to be perceived.'"

The fact that there was no actual Beatrice made the question even more interesting, philosophically.

"As the Spanish proverb says," I said, "'What the eyes do not see, the heart does not feel.'"

"Very true. At least I think so. And when I think of Cole Porter and the Letts, I also think of 'Let's Misbehave,' which also relates to the houses of ill fame. So you see, things come full circle, much like the course we have been following, and still are, as you can see."

"Yes, I see that." I glanced out the side window and saw our wake. We were making an aquamarine and white circle in the blue sea.

"I had considered coming to a stop while we made the repairs, but I was thinking of U boats. If there's another in the area, there's no sense giving him a stationary target. Well, the good news is that we're almost finished fixing the steering gear. I think we should be underway in a straight line by six o'clock tonight. Or, as you Navy boys like to put it, eighteen hundred hours."

"That's good."

"I see that you have posted a roving guard on the main deck."

"Yes, sir. There will be two men on guard at all times." Pancho and Lefty had drawn the first watch, and they were doing their rounds on deck as ordered, forty fives in their web belt holsters, shotguns cradled.

"Well, I suppose that's prudent," said the captain. "A lot of the crew are strangers. Who knows what they might get up to? After all, most of them were in jail. That suggests they'd done something illegal. Ha! Your men are armed, I see. Like the OK Corral."

"As you say—it's prudent."

"I saw a movie called *Frontier Marshall*. It was about Wyatt Earp. Played by Randolph Scott. Cesar Romero was his sidekick, Doc Holliday. Do you think that sort of thing really happened? That shootout at the OK Corral?"

"If it happened, it certainly didn't happen the way they played it in the movies."

"You didn't see it, then?"

"No. But I know that Hollywood movies and accurate history are strangers to each other."

Cesar Romero, for example, was certainly nothing like the real Doc Holliday, a tubercular, alcoholic dentist from Georgia. But Romero was under contract to the studio and had to play the roles bosses told him to. That was how it worked. Almost all the studio bosses came to Hollywood from the Old Country via lower Manhattan. They wouldn't know a quarter horse from a centipede. But they knew how to write a contract and how to enforce it. And they knew that most of the people in the audience didn't know the real history of anything any better than they did. So, they could say anything and produce whatever they thought would sell, and as long as the public liked it and bought the popcorn and Jujubes to go with it, everyone was happy. And it's easy to look down your nose at all of this, but like the captain's attitude toward cat houses, I didn't see all that much harm in it. It was just the movies, after all.

"So the movies don't tell the true history?" said the captain. "Really? Well, you would know about that, being from that part of the world. But in the great encyclopedia of mendacity known as human civilization, I don't suppose it matters very much. I do remember thinking at the time that the two of them seemed unlikely cowboys. Randolph Scott and Cesar Romero, I mean."

No more than Captain Flynn seemed like a *Boy's Life* image of a sea captain. He was Elmer Flynn, not Errol. But he was—a real captain, I mean. Had he really been in a shootout with actual banditos? That was hard to believe, too. But I didn't say anything. I could have asked him, but I'd rather believe he did. It was a better story. And I didn't bother telling him that Earp and Holliday weren't cowboys, just gamblers. I once ran into a guy who knew Earp when he lived in LA toward the end of his life. He told me Earp said LA was more crooked than Tombstone, Arizona. Well, that could very well be. I didn't know much about Tombstone, but I knew a lot about LA, including the cat houses. To tell the "honest truth," to use the captain's phrase, I didn't see anything wrong with them, either. You knew what you were getting going in, and you knew what you might take with you when you left. If that was OK with you, it was OK with me. It was conventionally immoral, of course, but I could live with it. I don't use those places, though—not because they're immoral, but because they're depressing. My Hollywood writer friend, Hobey Baker, says that I'm a romantic egoist. Maybe. But I prefer my women to be toward the ideal end of the human spectrum, as opposed to the still evolving. My experience with those places in LA was more in the line of detective work than as a customer. But I did know what they were like.

"I wonder if I should wear my Webley," Flynn said. "I don't think so. It's very heavy and drags my pants down. But if for some reason I need it, I know where I can put my hands on it quickly."

"Yes. That should be good enough."

Actually, the thought of the captain going around armed made me a little uncomfortable. I wasn't entirely convinced that he was . . . what? Completely sane? No, that was too strong. But he did seem just a little off center. All those lonely nights at sea, standing on the bridge with nothing to entertain him but his own thoughts? Did he really believe now and then that his Beatrice was real? If so, I was just as happy not having him walking around with a loaded forty-five pistol stuck in his belt. He might suddenly decide to take a shot at a seagull or, even worse, an albatross, and send a bullet into the hold or the ammunition locker by accident. And as every sailor knows, shooting at an albatross is a bad idea; hitting one is worse. Just ask the Ancient Mariner.

I went over to the chart table and looked at the course the captain had drawn. The line on the chart went just about due east. Along the way our only navigational job would be to take regular sun and star sightings to make sure weather and currents hadn't knocked us off course, and if they had, to make the necessary corrections. At night, we would darken ship, and at all times we'd maintain radio silence, except in case of emergencies. And as the days went by and we got farther into the vast emptiness of the Atlantic, an emergency signal wouldn't bring anyone's help anyway—wouldn't even be heard. So our best hope was for a voyage marked by silence and isolation. We'd be running at twelve knots, night and day. "Night and day." Cole Porter, again. Martha liked that song, too. I could just about hear her whispering. And, not for the first time, I had to smile about Captain Flynn's eccentricities. He was a little different, for sure, but when you got right down to it, most of us were.

I stared at the chart for a while. It was a hell of a big ocean, and I began to think about our security problem. I had to operate on the assumption that we had one—a security problem, I mean. After all, that's why I and the Fubars had been ordered here. If Bunny and his OSS buddies hadn't made a big issue out of it, I would never have given it a moment's thought. But they had. So I started reviewing the possible scenarios I had touched on with the Fubars. We had pretty much gone over the most likely plot—a bomb in the hold and escape by lifeboat. But how would it all work?

I decided to start from the beginning. If there were a saboteur on this bucket, he was obviously here to blow up the ship. So if I were that guy, how would I do it? And just as importantly, how would I plan to get away with my skin intact? Clearly, the key to escaping was the lifeboats. That meant there were probably at least two men in the plot, since *Carlota*'s boats had to be rowed. And they were big and heavy and not easy to lower from their davits down to the water. It would probably take two men to do it. A more modern ship would have power davits, and one man could lower a boat by himself. But not the elderly *Carlota*. You'd have to operate the ropes and pulleys on both ends of the boat. And once in the water, the boat would be unwieldy and difficult for one man to row. They were big and designed to hold dozens of passengers. Therefore, we were almost certainly dealing with at least two men. Maybe more. Since it would be impossible to lower a boat without being seen during the day, the saboteurs would have to act at night. They'd have to kill or incapacitate the two Fubars sometime after one o'clock in the morning, when almost the entire crew was asleep and the ship had no lights showing. No one would be on the bridge but the watch officer and the helmsmen, neither of whom could see very much in the darkness. And all of the lifeboats were hung abaft the bridge, on both sides of the ship. You couldn't even see them unless you made a point of going out on the wings of the bridge and looking aft. And there'd be almost no reason for the deck officer to do that. The noise of the ship's power plant and ventilators, the hum of electric devices, the wind and the action of the waves against the hull, the normal groaning and creaking of the ship being buffeted by the sea—all of it would probably muffle any sound of a boat being lowered. Once the saboteurs got rid of the Fubar guards, they could operate pretty safely. Unlike a Navy ship, a merchant ship like the *Carlota* almost never bothered with stationing lookouts, especially when the ship was in the middle of an empty ocean. They would swing a lifeboat out from the davits so that it was ready to be lowered to the water. Then they'd creep forward to the hold where the bulk of the cargo was stored. Now they would be below the bridge and the officer of the deck might be able to see them. But it would be dark and there would be almost no reason for the officer to notice a few shadows moving in the gloom. The helmsman would stand well back from the bridge's front windows. He couldn't see much more than the bow of the ship, even in the daylight.

There wasn't much doubt about how they planned to ignite the cargo. Simply starting a fire in the hold was too unpredictable. The ship could blow in minutes, or the fire might be extinguished somehow before anything happened. No, they would use a bomb with a time fuse of some sort. It could be a pocket-sized lump of plastic explosive with a pencil fuse stuck in it—or maybe even a classic time bomb with a clock taped to the explosive. It wouldn't have to be a very big bomb—just big enough to ignite the aviation gas or the ammunition. The cargo would do the serious work of destruction. In the dark the bombers would pry up a small piece of the corner of the hatch, and drop the plastic explosive into the hold. Then they'd scuttle back to the lifeboat, lower it, and row away. That meant the fuse or timer on the bomb would have to be long enough to let them get far enough away to be clear of the very impressive blast that *Carlota*'s exploding cargo would make. So start to finish, I figured they'd need a good half hour to get everything done and to get away without fear of getting too badly singed by the explosion. *Carlota* would be traveling at twelve knots. If they dropped directly astern and rowed in the opposite direction from *Carlota*'s course, they'd be several miles astern when she blew up.

But row away to where? Where would they go? As I looked at the chart there were only three possibilities—three sets of islands that were close enough to our course to allow the saboteurs to have a decent chance of making it to safety—Bermuda, the Azores, and Madeira. Of the three, Madeira with its harbor at Funchal was closest to the shores of North Africa. But really, any of them would do. If all went according to plan, there would be no survivors from the *Carlota*. In fact, there would be no *Carlota*. Not even much debris. What debris there was would be scattered for miles. The saboteurs could tell the authorities anything, and there'd be no one to contradict them. They could blame a U boat, or an accidental fire on board, or Moby bloody Dick. Then they could sit on the beach drinking rum until their employers came and picked them up. But for that all to work, they'd have to blow up the ship somewhere near one of those three island refuges. It would make no sense to do it in the middle of the Atlantic, a thousand miles from any landfall. And since the saboteurs were sympathetic to the Nazi cause—or at least allied with them temporarily, for political reasons—it figured that they'd want to destroy the ship closer to Europe. That's where they were much more likely to connect with friends. Bermuda might work, but it was a British island. Either the Azores or Madeira would be better. Both were owned by Portugal, and Portugal was neutral in the war. Hell, Lisbon was the destination of refugees from all over Europe and North Africa. It was the jumping-off point for North America. It was also a flea market of spies and double agents. Every side in the war had its agents there busily doing whatever they could do to frustrate each other and advance the cause of their handlers. The saboteurs could land on one of the Portuguese islands, receive the condolences of the local cops, jump a ship for Lisbon, and disappear into the arms of their employers—or their veiled houris and pigtailed Brunhildes.

That's how I'd do it, I thought. And the fact that it made so much sense and sounded not only feasible but almost easy gave me a queasy feeling in my stomach. The good news was—if I had this figured correctly—we would know where in general we'd have to be on special alert. When we were within lifeboat distance of the Portuguese island colonies, that was when they'd try it. And that was when we'd need to double the guard. With luck we'd have a surprise for them, and not the other way around. Even so, I would tell all the Fubars about the possibility of being attacked at any time and to stay together when making their rounds of the ship. I had wanted them to patrol individually to give us more constant surveillance of the key points in the ship. But I now thought it would be better to keep them together.

So much for the most obvious and logical plan for sabotage. There was another possibility, though. If the saboteur had a radio—one of those suitcase sets used by spies and resistance agents—he would have a way of contacting a U boat. He could call the U boat, give our position, and escape in a lifeboat while the U boat finished off *Carlota* with a deck gun or torpedo. That way he could get the job done anywhere in the mid ocean, because the U boat could then pick him, or them, up. That all seemed simple enough and feasible, but it was an easy contingency to prevent, because in order to do that, he would have to know *Carlota*'s exact position before he could tell the U boat where and when to show up. We could take care of that by locking the charts in the chart desk and only bringing them out when we took celestial readings and corrected our position on the chart. And no one could break into the chart desk without being seen by the officer on watch—the captain, the first mate, or me. Of course, he could tell the U boat that we were steering 090 or something, but that wouldn't be enough information. We could be anywhere along that line. U boats operated by visual contact, and with the curvature of the earth going for us, they couldn't see much beyond ten miles. They might see our smoke, but not at night, and they wouldn't see our lights because we'd be darkened. There was talk that the U boats were developing long-range radar to help in spotting targets beyond the visual range, but so far the word was they hadn't got it. So I would talk to the captain and the first mate about locking up our charts and keeping our position a matter of conversation only between us. I'd also have the Fubars keep an eye out for a suitcase radio. The ship's radio room was just behind the bridge, so that would be no problem. Anyone trying to send a signal from there would be spotted by the watch officer. Besides we were sailing in radio silence, so if anyone tried to send a signal, he'd be noticed immediately.

The more I thought about it, the more it seemed likely that he'd use a bomb, even if that was originally a backup plan, when he realized he couldn't signal a U boat with our position.

There was only one other scenario that I could think of—a suicide saboteur. And unfortunately there wasn't very much we could do about that. Having posted the regular watch of guards, and having alerted the Fubars to the danger, and having told them to them watch the crew, we had done about all that we could do to prevent someone from committing suicide for the greater glory of the Fuhrer. But I couldn't take the idea very seriously. You might kill yourself over a woman or bad debts. Back during the Crash of '29 guys were jumping out of their Wall Street office windows, but I think more than a few of them had second thoughts on the way down. You certainly wouldn't do something like that over politics. Would you?

Thinking of suicide reminded me of Nietzsche, Hitler's favorite lunatic. Nietzsche said that the thought of suicide is a great comfort and helps you get through a very bad night. At least I think it was Nietzsche. If not him, it was some other screwball. I don't know what was troubling Nietzsche's nights. But since Hitler seems to have taken a liking to his theories, it's too bad Nietzsche didn't take his own advice and end it all. He could have done the world a favor and saved the rest of us a lot of trouble by tearing up his Superman manuscript and checking out permanently.

Speaking of the Nazi supermen, Martha told me she met one of them at an embassy reception before the war. Heinrich Himmler. She said he couldn't see three feet in front of him without his glasses, and his breath could wilt a cactus.

Chapter Eleven

After dinner I went to the bridge. It was just that time of fading light when the stars were coming out, but you could still see the horizon. That was the time for taking a star sighting and fixing the ship's position. You did that by using a sextant to measure the angles of a few reliable stars. It was a problem in spherical geometry. I remembered studying celestial navigation in officer training, and the first time I worked out a solution to a classroom problem, my calculations located my "ship" somewhere high and dry in the Catskill Mountains of New York, not in Long Island Sound, which was the correct school solution. But over time I got better at it. You took the measure of at least three stars by locating them in the sextant optics and then moving them down to the horizon with the sextant's protractor-like device that marked the angle of each. Then you consulted the tables, and when you had the information about those stars' positions for that day, you drew the angles on the chart, and where those lines intersected was your position. You knew where you were because the heavens said so. It was very satisfying, when the lines all crossed at exactly the same point. It had to make you smile for a number of reasons. There you were, a human microbe in a microbe of a vessel, alone on an endless sea, asserting not only that you were a part of the universe, but also that your position in it was precisely here on this imaginary spot on the water. There might be lost souls in the world, but you were not one of them. Well done. But at those times I also thought of the lines from Steven Crane—"*The man said to the Universe, 'Sir I exist!' And the Universe replied, 'Yes, but that does not create in me a sense of obligation.'*" That might not be the exact quote, but it's close enough—much like my star plots. Celestial navigation made you feel cosmically insignificant and at the same time pleased with yourself for being able to use the stars that way. For that brief moment, they were your tools. You asked them a question, and they were made to answer. Their light had started their travels to you a thousand light years ago, just to do you this favor, or so it seemed. The star that had sent that light might not even exist anymore, might have burnt out or exploded a million years ago. But you were using the last of its light to find and mark your position. Then, necessarily, the ship continued to move and so did the stars, so that your brief moment of self-assertion, knowledge, and mastery was exactly that—brief. And if that didn't make you smile ruefully and wryly, well, you were missing a big part of the experience. The whole thing was a metaphor, of course—a complicated one, to be sure, but they're usually the best kind.

The first mate was on watch, and unlike the captain, who resembled an egg in both shape and hairlessness, First Mate Timmons did look the part of a storybook sailor. He was tanned and fit looking with clear blue eyes and a wind-burned complexion. As I said before—central casting. He was in his usual white sweater and dark pants. He had a jaunty officer's hat covering his blond mane. Like most salty sailors he wore no stiffening grommet in his hat, and the sides flopped down over the hatband. Very stylish. I had adopted the same style after I had been promoted to lieutenant. Doing it before then would have risked the snickers of my men. But I was getting close to legitimate professional saltiness. The gold band on my everyday hat was turning nicely green.

Timmons was standing on the port wing of the bridge and preparing to take his sightings, too. It was a calm evening with just the hint of a breeze. We would have a clear horizon and a steady platform. We should be able to get good readings. I remembered that my skipper on the *Nameless* used to say that people pay forty dollars a day to cruise around like this, and "here we were getting paid to do it." He was joking, but he meant it, too. Well, I could understand. It was a beautiful evening, and the sea ahead was smooth, and the light off the water looked like it was made of something soft.

Timmons was whistling a tune that sounded familiar.

"What's the name of that song?" I asked him, after we'd exchanged friendly greetings.

"Oh, it's something by Vera Lynn. Our national treasure. She has the voice of an angel, don't you agree?"

"Yes, I do."

"The song is called 'The Nightingales Sang on Berkeley Square.'"

"Yes. I remember hearing it."

"I sometimes wonder whether Berkeley Square was named after the philosopher we were talking about earlier." He looked at me and smiled, slyly. "It reminds me of something I once read about something someone said. I can't remember who it was. Brainy sort of cove. He was writing about the ancient Greeks, and he said, '*The* Iliad *and the* Odyssey *were written by Homer, but if not by Homer, then by someone with that same name.*' Ha! I think the same could be said of Berkeley Square."

"Maybe it was named after a man named Square."

"Eh? Oh. Ha, ha! Good one. I never thought of that. It could very well be. There was a character named Square in *Tom Jones*, as I remember. Got caught in a strumpet's closet with his pants around his ankles. He was a philosopher, too. Have you read it? *Tom Jones*?"

"Yes. A while ago."

"I identify with the main character. Both of us expelled for boyish high spirits. You know, I often quote that line about Homer, and I find there are two kinds of people in the world—those who think it's funny and those who stare at you and decide after a while that there's something wrong with you. I was glad to see you smile about it. Life is too short to associate with people who have no sense of humor, don't you think?"

"As a matter of fact, I do. My Navy skipper once said something along the same lines. Of course, sometimes we have no choice."

"Sad, but true."

"That story reminds me of something my skipper once told me. He said he knew a guy named Fred who had a dog named Fred, and when my skipper asked him why he named the dog after himself, the guy said he didn't. He named it after his father."

"Ha! Good one. Your captain has a taste for absurdity."

"Yes, he does. He says it tastes good."

While we were talking, Timmons was also expertly sighting the appropriate stars with his sextant, measuring the angles and writing his readings in a notebook. "Arcturus is my favorite star," he said. "I like the name. If I ever had a son, I think I would call him Arcturus. Having a name like that would make life difficult for him, poor little chap. But life is not all beer and skittles and time in bed with Sally Free. Speaking of Berkeley Square and nightingales, have you ever actually heard one of those birds singing?"

"No. I don't think we have them in the US."

"It's no loss. For the life of me I can't figure out what's the big attraction. Poets and that sort are always going on and on about their beautiful song. To me they sound like they're doing quite a lot of stammering, rather like our beloved King George. But if you believe the Bard, the nightingale is some kind of symbol of love. I suppose that's because he stammers and sings at night. The bird, not the Bard. Ha, ha. What's that line from *Romeo and Juliet*?" He paused for a moment and looked out over the ocean. "I know—Juliet and Romeo are just waking up after a night of love making and Romeo starts getting out of bed, so Juliet says—*Wilt thou be gone? It is not yet near day. It was the nightingale and not the lark that peirc'd the fearful hollow of thine ear. Nightly she sings on yon pomegranate tree; believe me love, it was the nightingale.*"

"Very good. I'm impressed."

"Yes. I don't blame you. I was paying attention in that class, as well as philosophy. I was really rather a good student, despite Doctor Grimes's irrational prejudice against me in general and drunken fornication in particular. Or maybe the other way round. Suffice it to say he didn't approve of either. But I quite liked Shakespeare. That's Juliet talking, the minx. She wants Romeo to stay. He knows better. He says, '*It was the lark, the herald of the morn, no nightingale.*' But of course the woman always does want a bit of a cuddle afterward, when the man is just as happy to put on his cod piece and be gone. It's one of the differences between the two, don't you agree?"

"I know what you mean." That reminded me of something Martha told me when we first met—that she only indulged in sex to get a little tenderness afterward. In fact, at the time she told me she really wasn't all that fond of sex. It was just a means to an end, and she basically just put up with it, hoping it would be over soon. I'm happy to say she has changed her mind about that, and if she gives me some of the credit for her change of heart, well, I can live with it.

"But Romeo's afraid he'll be discovered," I said. "He believes he's in mortal danger."

"Yes. That's what he says. But he would say that, wouldn't he, the rascal. I think he probably just needed to pee. And it wouldn't be terribly romantic to let fly into the chamber pot, after having spent those tender hours with Juliet. This was only their first night together, I think. If not the first, then certainly it was still early in their affair. A month or so later, he might not have been so shy."

"And going off the balcony wouldn't be much better."

"No. That would have given a whole new meaning to 'The Balcony Scene.' Even worse—there could have been a gardener down there, doing some early morning weeding. And it's hard to get a good gardener. Believe me, you don't want to offend them. Old Doctor Grimes had one at the school who was notorious for the very sins that got me tossed out. But students, especially ones on scholarship, are easy to come by; gardeners are not. Anyway, nightingales aside, it's still a pretty song—Vera Lynn's, I mean. I think she's wonderful. Have you ever noticed that a woman who can sing transforms herself into a beauty simply by opening her mouth and breaking into song?"

"Yes, I have." I didn't think Reynolds would agree with me, though, at least not as far as the Andrews Sisters were concerned. But I did think that was true in general, although, let's be honest, Kate Smith could stand to lose a few pounds.

"It certainly works for Vera Lynn," said Timmons. "Objectively speaking, she's nobody's Venus on a Clam Shell. But she's transformed when she sings."

"I know what you mean."

"But do you think it works the other way around? What about a beautiful and desirable girl who has a voice like the captain's parrot," Timmons said. "What happens when *she* starts to sing?"

"I'll bite."

"Nothing! She's still beautiful and desirable! Ha, ha!"

"I thought the captain's parrot never says anything."

"No, he doesn't. He is what you might call circumspect. But if he did talk or sing, I assume he would sound like any other parrot. A series of squawks and screeches. Not very pretty. I had a cousin like Cato. He never said a word until he was five years old. His parents thought he was simple minded. But one day at dinner he said quite clearly, 'Please pass the salt.' Up until that time, he hadn't wanted for anything and was content to let things go along as they were. He's now an Oxford don. Very brainy, like that Homer cove. Wrote a book on rhetoric—my cousin, that is. He's well known for the brevity of his lectures."

"So you think it's possible that Cato will say something one day?"

"I think it's very possible. But you never know about parrots. Unlike nightingales. Apparently, *they* never shut up."

We finished taking our sightings of the stars and working through the calculations, and our solutions were just about the same. The *Carlota* had been traveling east for a couple of hours now, and she had not drifted off the line the captain had drawn on the chart. Well, as I said, it was a calm day. How well *Carlota* would maintain her course in rough weather remained to be seen.

"So far so good," said Timmons.

I had talked to the captain at dinner about keeping the charts locked away, and I mentioned it to Timmons now.

"Good idea," he said. "Can't have the Wogs knowing where they are. They might realize they don't need us to get them back to dry land. Are you going to take the midwatch?"

"Yes." The midwatch was midnight to four. It was most officers' least favorite, for obvious reasons. But I didn't mind. It was generally the quietest, and as long as things went smoothly, you were not disturbed by the ship's regular routines. It was a good time to think. Besides, I had arranged this so that Ali would be my helmsman. It would be a good way to get to know him. Or, rather, observe him.

"Good. Well, then I'll see you later. It was good of you to volunteer. Otherwise, the captain and I would be worn down with care and fatigue at the end of the voyage."

"Glad to do it. But what you do you do under normal circumstances?"

"Oh, there was a second mate who stood watch, of course. He disappeared with most of the crew, although he said he had a good reason. Something about his wife and the local minister. These things happen all the time. A sailor who is married is asking for that sort of difficulty, unless he has more than one wife. That takes some planning and schedule management, of course, but I've known some chaps who made it work. That way when one wife runs off with the local parson, there's another waiting in the wings. Or in Liverpool. The second mate's problem was that he was monogamous by nature. He was quite broken up when he got the letter containing the bird."

"The bird?"

"You know, 'I've met someone else, but I hope we can still be friends. No hard feelings.' That sort of thing."

"Ah, yes. That bird."

"You know that Oscar Wilde said that bigamy was one wife too many and monogamy was the same thing. Clever chap, but his knowledge of sailors is very limited. That's rather surprising when you think of it. But really it's the other way around for a sailor, assuming he wants to be married. The more the merrier, within reason. That way when one wife runs off, it's not so distressing. Speaking of that, did you know that penguins were monogamous?"

"Yes, I read that somewhere."

"Well, it's not surprising, when you think of it. They all look alike, so what's the point of switching? By the way, I'm glad to see you have arranged for your men to be on guard. Can't take too many precautions with military cargo. We're a civilian ship, after all. Can't let the side down."

"That is true."

"Well, see you at midnight. If you hear any nightingales singing, you will know that I have taken a very wrong turn somewhere."

I went down the starboard ladder to the main deck. I had heard the joke about the penguins before, but it still made me smile. What did Timmons say about Romeo? That he was a rascal? Apparently, Timmons would know.

Otto and Reynolds were on watch as guards.

"All quiet?" I said, unnecessarily.

"Yes, sir."

"Have you guys picked up on anything funny about the crew? Anything at all?"

Though the Fubars were enjoying life in the passenger cabins, they took their meals on the mess deck with the rest of the crew.

"No, sir. They're just a bunch of guys. I don't think many of them knew each other before signing on here."

I could believe that. While we were still repairing the steering gear the captain had mustered the rest of the crew on the main deck. He told them he wanted to give them some information about the voyage, but the real reason was to give me a chance to look them over. I didn't know what I expected to see, but it was just one more stone to turn over. As Reynolds said, they were a motley looking collection of foreigners—a couple of Filipinos, the usual handful of Lascars, some South Americans, a Swede and a Danish guy, the Lett who was the captain's helmsman, Ali, and a few Europeans from the Balkans. Standing there, they didn't show any resentment for being called together, no resentment for being legally shanghaied, no resentment of the ship's officers, no particular worries about the nature of the cargo and the danger of the mission. They were neither friendly nor sullen. There was nothing about them that was in any way furtive or even slightly alarming. Nothing. Just a mixed bag of guys.

Flynn and Timmons and I had agreed beforehand to tell the crew that we would catch up to the convoy. There'd be no mention of sailing alone. It seemed to me a useful deception. After all, I had been sent there along with the Fubars in part to keep an eye on the crew. They had been snatched from the Norfolk jail, most of them, and there was the possibility that they might do more than grumble about spending the next two weeks aboard a floating bomb, all alone, dodging U boats. I didn't like it much myself, so I could imagine what they might feel. It was highly unlikely that they would do anything about it. Mutiny was rare. So what was the risk of the deception? None. It was a different version of "*What the eyes do not see, the heart does not feel.*" So we all agreed on it. I had already told the Fubars not to say anything about anything; I was not worried about them. It also occurred to me that if we did have a saboteur on board, he might decide to wait until we had rejoined the convoy to set off his bomb. If he was a thinking agent, he would realize that it would give his clients maximum bang for their bucks. In fact it would just be the original plan delayed by however long it took us to catch up. What's more he could escape to one of the undamaged ships, and it would be a lot easier than rowing to some distant island.

"Okay. Anything else, guys?"

"The only thing that seems a little funny," said Otto, "is that the big blond guy from somewhere in Russia or someplace—"

"Patkul?"

"Yes, sir. He and that Arab or whatever he is, Ali. They seem to be buddies. I only mention it because they look like Mutt and Jeff together. One is big and blond and white and the other one is small and dark and not so white. More of an off-white."

"Do they seem to have any sort of attitude? Any gripes."

"No, sir. They're both pretty nice guys. Nice and friendly to everybody. It's just that they look kind of unusual together, you might say."

"Sort of like you and Kate Smith, sir," said Reynolds.

.

Chapter Twelve

The French and Spanish had divided up Morocco, although the French ended up with the bigger part. The Spanish had the north, though, and the city of Tangier, a very active trading port. They were looking across the Straits of Gibraltar at the detested English Rock, which they believed rightfully belonged to Spain, but didn't. Six or so years ago, when Franco and his buddies decided they had enough of the so-called Republic in Spain—a ferret cage of squabbling liberals, socialists, anarchists, and communists—he joined with some other generals to restore the traditional order, meaning the usual collection of interested parties—the land-owning aristocracy and the Church. All that is common knowledge, I suppose. The results were a horrific civil war. Most civil wars are particularly nasty—a lot of neighbors settling scores and a lot of zealots organizing firing squads. But Spain was particularly bad. I know because Martha covered the war, and she told me some of the stuff that went on. I had also read Hemingway's book about the war. I thought it was particularly fine, and it sold well, too. Martha was fierce in her opinions about the rightness and wrongness and who were the good guys, although from what I could tell, there weren't many of those on either side. Like most of the Western journalists reporting on the war, she hated Franco and his gang, and she tended to overlook or excuse the vicious antics of the Republicans. She was there with Hemingway. They weren't married then and were having a test run, I think, to determine whether a more official, long-term arrangement made sense. Well, even in those early days of their affair, she was grinning and bearing it and wishing it would get over with quickly. So that should have given her a clue. Him, too, in fairness. But you can talk yourself into just about anything, if you try hard enough. For some reason they both wanted to buy what they were selling to themselves, so they did. In the beginnings of our love affair, I felt kind of uneasy hearing anything about her private life. But she said her coldness and lack of interest in her marriage was nothing personal. She had felt that way with other men in her life, too. It wasn't anyone's fault. Well, it still wasn't any of my business, but I could live with it, especially since she told me a lot of it while we were locked together in a sleeping bag, under the stars, on a beach in Cuba. Neither one of us was cold then.

Anyway, I had always found it ironic that when Franco brought his army to Spain and more or less started the civil war, he left from Morocco. His buddy Hitler gave him and his North African army a ride across the Straits. Both the German navy and Luftwaffe helped ferry them to Spain. Most of Franco's army consisted of Moors. The irony is, these Moors were descendants of the same people who'd been kicked out of Spain by Queen Isabella—the same Isabella who had a soft spot for Columbus. She was trying to purify Spain and eliminate any non-Catholic groups who might have a skeptical word to say about the Church, or who might feel that there were other paths to Salvation than the one dictated by the Pope and his priests. I think Isabella's husband Ferdinand had a hand in this business, too. This was about the same time they introduced the Inquisition, so times were hard for anyone with divergent views. That included the Moors and the Jews. So they were all packed up and sent to Morocco and points south. And now the Moors were being welcomed back as a rescuer of the royalists and Catholic Church. Quite a laugh to the casual observer. No one was asking the Jews to come back, though. That was no surprise. Even they seemed to believe that their role in history was to be eternal outcasts, though they weren't sure why.

I was thinking about all this as I was getting ready to go on watch. It seemed a possible side door into a discussion of politics with Ali. I was interested in his attitude toward the French in Morocco, but I thought, if he were someone we'd need to keep careful eye on—if he were a potential saboteur, to put it plainly—his political ideas about European colonialism might give some indication. But rather than ask him directly about how he felt about the French, I'd go at it by mentioning the Spanish. To an Arab, there would be very little difference between them, in principle. Both were there in Morocco. Both were resented by the Arab majority. The war that the Arabs had fought twenty years ago was against both the French and the Spanish. And I knew from my previous assignment that there was a very active native resistance effort that had made a deal with the devil, that is, the Germans, in the hopes of eventually expelling the French. Whether or not this was another version of the King Stork story was something the locals preferred to think about later. And I very much doubt that the Moorish politicians behind these antics gave much thought to the fact that the main characters in the King Stork fable were frogs. But I thought it was kind of funny.

At quarter to twelve, or 2345 I should say, I went up to relieve Timmons on the bridge. That was the Navy way. You got to your watch fifteen minutes before the top of the hour. And don't be late. I didn't know if the merchant fleet used the same rules, but I wasn't going to violate naval tradition.

Timmons was glad to see me.

"It's been a long day," he said. "I'm ready to 'knit up the raveled sleeve of care.'"

"Anything doing?"

"No. No contacts. Weather's good. Course 090, all ahead standard, steaming as before."

All ahead standard was twelve knots on *Carlota*.

I checked the radar scope for contacts. There were none. We had the radar stretched out to its maximum range, which was about ten miles. I walked out on the starboard wing of the bridge and looked around for lights. There were none. I checked the port wing. No lights. Everything was quiet, except for the humming and clanking and groaning of *Carlota* and the hissing and splashing of the bow wave. But you didn't really hear those sounds unless you tried to. Otherwise, they were just the usual background.

"Very well. I relieve you, sir," I said.

"Thank you. I'll just make a note in the log and toddle off to bed."

While this was going on Ali arrived and took over the helm from a
Swede named Olaf. Then Olaf and Timmons left, and I was alone with
Ali. He looked over and nodded. I think he smiled, but it was too dark
in there to be sure. There were almost no lights on the bridge, and those
that were necessary were shielded—primarily the binnacle for the helmsman, so that he could see his compass course. There was another compass
just below the front windows, so that the watch officer could verify the
helmsman's course. Next to the wheel was the engine order telegraph
that was used to signal engine speed changes to the engine room. It was
brass and I was pleased to see that it was well polished. There was a slight
green glow from our primitive radar screen. It was shaded on three sides
and visible only from the rear. Our radar was almost useless, except to
spot contacts that were fairly close. It was an antiquated system, but it
was better than nothing. As the strobe swung in its endless circle, no blips
appeared. The chart table was clear, because we had locked our charts
away. Besides, we had taken our last sightings at twilight and there was
no other way on this ship to locate our position and see if, or rather how
far, we had drifted off our plotted course. That would have to wait until
morning when the horizon appeared and stars were still visible. In short,
the bridge was almost completely dark. I looked down toward the main
deck. I wanted to see if I could see the Fubars moving around down there.
But everything was still. No movement that I could see. The moon had
set and the stars were a little shrouded by high clouds. Even so, I could
see the white bow wave as we rose and fell very moderately.

I went back out to the starboard wing of the bridge to sniff the night
air. Looking behind, I could watch the white turbulence of our wake. I
could see it pretty clearly from there. It was straight and well defined.
A straight wake meant a competent helmsman. I always thought it was
also a useful metaphor. It marked very clearly where you have been and
suggested that you have traveled intelligently, whereas the dark sea ahead
told you little or nothing about the future. And if, now and then, it told
you anything at all, it was likely to be troubling—storms or shoals or
waterspouts or rogue waves or any number of possible disasters waiting
for you at sea. There were no lines ahead to mark where you should go.
Those lines were only in your head. And so we plowed forward in the

dark. I think my Hollywood friend Hobey wrote something like that in one of his books that nobody read. Well, I read them, but I was in the very small minority.

Metaphors aside, I always enjoyed watching the wake. Even though I could see it pretty well from the bridge wing, I knew that the fantail on this or any ship is a much better place to watch it. You stand all the way aft and look straight down on the changing colors and the endlessly fascinating motion of the water as it's churned up by the ship's propellers. And if you're really lucky at least one time in your life, maybe you get to do this on an elegant transatlantic liner. And in the best of all possible worlds, you do this in the company of a beautiful woman you just met in the ship's bar. And maybe the evening is a little cool, so that you can offer her your white dinner jacket to drape over her bare shoulders, since her evening gown is strapless and low cut. And ideally on that evening, the stars are out in the kind of profusion you can only find at sea, which gives you the chance to mention, with some sense of wonder, how people use them to navigate across vast oceans. Maybe you point out some of the brighter ones and tell her the name of one or two. And then she asks you if you are a sailor, and you nod modestly and say, yes. If you smoke, it's also a good time to offer her a cigarette. I don't smoke, but I have seen how this plays in the movies. It always seems to work out well and lead to something.

Yes, that's the best way to watch a ship's wake. Watching *Carlota's* was more than a little short of the romantic ideal. But it was still a pretty scene, even from the bridge wing of a rusted banana boat, and even though the nearest beautiful woman was a couple of hundred miles away and getting farther away every second. *What'll I do when you are far away?* That's easy—imagine.

After a while I went back into the pilot house where Ali was at the wheel. He smiled and nodded as I went by. The rules of etiquette in these situations are that the officer on watch will determine whether there's any conversation. If he wants to spend four hours in total silence apart from orders to the helm and engine room, then that's his prerogative. But if he wants to talk he merely has to make some observation or ask a question. At that point, most enlisted men will take the hint and answer. Most of them like to talk. The hours on watch can be long and more than a few sailors are naturally garrulous anyway. That's why they're generally such good company.

So I said to Ali—

"Have you been going to sea for a long time, Ali?"

"Oh not so very long, sir," he said, flashing a grin. He had a Middle Eastern accent that I will not try to reproduce. Accents and dialects on the printed page are almost always tedious to read, except in books by Mark Twain or Dickens. And even they can get a little old after a while. My eyes had gotten better adjusted to the gloom, so even in the dim light I could see him well enough. He was small and slight and had a bushy mane of black hair, a straggly beard that suggested neglect rather than intentional fashion, and an open and friendly expression. He seemed like someone who was willing, almost eager, to please. "I was in the army before," he said. "But it didn't suit me, so I went to sea and became an AB after a while. I like it pretty well." AB meant able-bodied seaman, which was a step up from a simple deck hand.

"Army, huh?"

"Yes, sir. The Spanish Foreign Legion, actually."

"Really? Were you in for a long time? I heard you had to sign up for a minimum of seven years." I think I remembered this from seeing Beau Geste. But of course that was the French Foreign Legion. The Spanish Legion might be different.

"Five years, sir. But it didn't suit me, so I left a few years early. Four and a half years early, to be exact."

"How did you manage that?" I was pretty sure he didn't just put in a polite request.

"I buggered off."

"Deserted."

"That's the legal term, yes, sir."

"I understand the discipline in the Legion is harsh."

"Yes, sir. But it wasn't that so much. The Spanish officers were alright. You didn't really see much of them. The sergeants and corporals did most of the work. And many of them were Moors, too. They were the real bastards. Give some men stripes on their sleeves, and they change. Or should I say, the real them comes to the surface."

"Oh. Yes, I know what you mean. And so you went to sea?"

"Yes, sir. It seemed the best way to avoid the military police. I went back to Casablanca, where I was born. I met my wife there and got a job on a freighter. I didn't want to leave her, but it was the only job I could find. So . . . here I am."

"You're new to *Carlota*, aren't you?"

"Yes, sir. I joined in Norfolk, along with most of the others. Most of them were taken from the jail, but I was wandering around the docks looking for a new ship to sign on with. The one I arrived on paid off the crew before going into dry dock. I heard the *Carlota* was looking for men, and so there you have it. Viola, as the French say."

"And Voila, too."

"Oh, yes. That's the word. Ha, ha! My mistake. It can be difficult for an Arabic speaker to learn European languages quickly. Everything is so different."

"I can believe it. But you speak English very well."

"Thank you, sir. It is easier, I find, than French. My mother was Sephardic, and she placed very great importance on speaking English. She said it is the language of business, and we had better learn it. My father was a merchant, so he naturally agreed."

"Was he Sephardic, too? I assume so."

"No, sir. He was a Moor. I am half and half."

The Sephardic were descendants of the Iberian Jews who were exiled by Isabella. They had spread around the Mediterranean, but many had stayed in Morocco. It occurred to me that with Ali's Iberian heritage, he should have no trouble with Spanish and therefore with other romance languages. But maybe the centuries had wiped away any traces of Spanish from his mother's people. I didn't know. But I did know their Hebraic language was different from the Yiddish of the Ashkenazi Jews who were from Russia, Poland, and Germany, mostly. They were two different people joined only by a common religion and a tradition of persecuted wandering. I learned all this on my last assignment in Casablanca. Till then I had never heard of the Sephardic. There were plenty of Jews in

Hollywood, but they were almost entirely first or second generation immigrants from Eastern Europe and therefore Ashkenazi. I also wondered about the possibility of a Moor marrying a Sephardic woman. I had the impression that the Moors and the Jews didn't get along. But they had been living side by side for five centuries in Morocco, so maybe they had learned to tolerate each other. I did know the Arabs and Jews lived in different neighborhoods. Casablanca, for example, was rigidly segregated. So Ali's parents seemed like an unusual match. But maybe not.

"Are your parents still alive?" I said.

"Sadly, no. I lost them both."

Inevitably, I thought of the old Oscar Wilde line—"To lose one parent may be regarded as misfortune; to lose both looks like carelessness." But of course I didn't say it.

"Did this happen while you were still a child?"

"Yes. Still a boy. My father killed my mother in a fit of jealousy. He was told she was having an affair with the local rabbi, but it was a foul lie. She was innocent, but my father lost his head and smothered her with a pillow. Moors can be violent, now and then. The French arrested him and sent him to the guillotine. People said he lost his head twice, but I don't think that was very funny."

"No, I don't suppose it is. It's a sad story."

"Yes. To me, it was a tragedy."

I wondered. Was Ali serious? He was very matter of fact about everything. He didn't seem resentful. The French had executed his father, and he could hardly believe it wasn't justified. Still, it was a little odd that he seemed to accept things so easily. As for the story—a jealous Moor kills his wife after a false accusation of infidelity? Really? As the tune goes—*it seems to me I've heard this song before.*

"But you are happy going to sea?"

"I am happy not to be a soldier, sir. For a while I was stationed in Spain during the troubles there. I wasn't there long, but it was long enough to see some terrible things. The country was filled with all sorts of different people—not just the different Spanish political parties, but Italians and Germans and Russians and so on. Very brutal. Everyone killing everyone else."

"Yes, I have heard it was very bad there."

"You cannot imagine how bad, sir. The truth is, I am a poet, and the sights of war and the cruelty of man to man upset me."

"A poet? That explains it. I noticed that you were talking to yourself yesterday while you were on watch. Were you reciting?"

"Not exactly, sir. I was composing." It was clear we had hit on Ali's enthusiasm, for he brightened up considerably. "Poetry is made to be heard, not just read, and the poet should say the words out loud to be sure that what he thinks is a poem is actually something of value."

"Makes sense."

"Arabic poetry is very interesting," he said, "because it is just as beautiful when it is written as when it is spoken. Our calligraphy is very elegant, so a written poem is both picture and a sound at once. Or it can be either. Would you like to hear something of mine?"

"I'm afraid I don't know Arabic."

"Oh, not to worry, as Mr. Timmons likes to say. I will translate it for you."

"Well, then, okay," I said, without too much enthusiasm.

He composed himself to recite.

"I call this one 'Ah, That Sweet Spring!'

Ah, that sweet spring should vanish with the rose,
That youth's sweet scented manuscript should close,
The nightingale that in the branches sang,
Ah, whence, and whither flown again, who knows?"

There was that bird again, I thought.

He looked at me hopefully.

"Very good," I said. "I don't know much about such things, but I would encourage you to keep up with it."

"It sounds better in Arabic."

"I can believe it. Not that I don't like it in English."

"I'm glad. I have others."

"Are they all equally short?"

"Oh, yes, sir. I work in quatrains with an AABA rhyme scheme. For example, this one I call 'The Worldly Hope':

The worldly hope set their hopes upon
Turns ashes, or it prospers, and anon,
Like snow upon the desert's dusty face
Lighting an hour or two—is gone.

You see?"

"Yes. And it seems amazing to me that your rhyme scheme works in English as well as Arabic. That is, I assume it works in Arabic."

"Oh, yes, sir. And you're correct. It's not easy to find two words in different languages that mean the same thing and also rhyme in the same way. That's why I work in only four lines. A longer poem would be very difficult. But what do you think? Is there an interest in America in poetry? I sometimes dream of going there and making my fortune."

"I see. Well, you wouldn't be the first to think of trying it. And, yes, there's a company called Hallmark that publishes this kind of thing. You might want to contact them." You also might want to tamp down the gloom and world weariness, I thought—especially for Get Well cards.

"Truly? That is very good to know. Thank you, sir."

Well, why not, I thought. Why shouldn't Ali go to America and reinvent himself as the Wordsworth of the greeting card business? That was the American way. One of the things I always found interesting about Hollywood was that nearly everyone who was there started out as someone else from somewhere else. There was nothing wrong with that, as long as you didn't fool yourself into believing your new biography, especially if it was written by the studio publicity department. But Hollywood was the embodiment of the American dream of self-reinvention. The only difference was that compared to the rest of the country, Hollywood was operating at twice the RPM and half the authenticity. That's why almost everyone was always nervous.

And then I started to wonder—if Ali genuinely was an aspiring poet who was shocked and sickened by scenes of war in Spain, was he likely to be an enemy operative who was a danger to the ship and to our mission?

Could he have been recruited to be an enemy agent? Ali? A rather slight and friendly little man with nothing remotely sinister about him? A man who seemed to bear no ill will toward the Europeans who were occupying his country?

And once again the answer was—well, why not? If you were a German operative recruiting Arabs for sabotage, you wouldn't select a guy with a jeweled turban and wearing a golden scimitar stuck in a silk sash. You'd choose someone who looked like everyone else, only less so, someone you wouldn't notice even if you were staring at him in an otherwise empty room. In other words, you'd choose a guy exactly like Ali. Maybe you met him while he was in Spain. Maybe you arranged for his discharge, because you had plans for him, and you and the Wehrmacht were helping out your ally, the Spanish army, and so they were willing to cooperate. Or maybe he really was a deserter, and you recruited him only a few days ago in Norfolk. In either case, you'd give him some phony story borrowed from Shakespeare and a few lines of cheesy verse, no doubt taken from somewhere else. Then you'd pat him on the head, give him a lump of plastic explosive, a tiny detonator fuse, and send him on his way with your best wishes. If he made a mistake and blew himself up, well, so what—as long as he got the ship, too. And even if he didn't, what was one ragged Arab, more or less? It was no skin off your nose. You could say to yourself, "Nice try, Fritz, old boy. Can't win 'em all. Go find another one and try again."

On the other hand, there's the theory called Occam's razor, which says that the simplest explanation of any sort of question is likely to be the correct one. And the simplest explanation here was that Ali was nothing more than what he seemed to be. *Esse est percepi?* Well, as they say in the Saturday matinee serials, to be continued.

CHAPTER THIRTEEN

AT 4 A.M. CAPTAIN FLYNN CAME ON TO THE BRIDGE TO RELIEVE ME. Apparently he didn't subscribe to Navy traditions about getting there early. Patkul also arrived and took over the wheel from Ali without any ceremony.

"Good, morning, Lieutenant," Flynn said. "Everything ticking over in good shape?"

"Yes, sir. No contacts, steaming as before, course 090, all ahead standard. Barometer steady."

He took a look around from both wings of the bridge, checked the compass and the radar, and looked at the chart table, out of habit.

"Very well. I relieve you, sir. Isn't that what you Navy blokes say?"

"Yes, sir."

"Good on ya, cobber. That's what we say down under." He pronounced it "Undah."

I went down the ladder to the main deck to check on the Fubars. Williams and Smithers had just come on watch. They had both traded their white Navy caps for dark blue wool watch caps, and in their work dungarees, they were practically invisible in the darkness.

"All quiet, guys?" I said, unnecessarily.

"Yes, sir. Nothing stirring."

"All right. Carry on. I'm going to hit the rack for a couple of hours. Good night."

In the morning I went up to the bridge to take a sighting. Timmons was on watch again. He had already taken the fix of the ship's position.

"Only wandered two miles off course," he said. "Easily corrected. Must have been some wind toward the end of the night, although the skipper didn't mention anything."

"I don't suppose I need to take a reading, then."

"Only if you want the practice, old boy. Have you heard the latest? Cato is missing."

"Really? How does the captain feel about that?"

"He's delighted. He says maybe Cato has run off to join a flock of seagulls. Although strictly speaking he would have flown off, not run. If so, I expect we'll see him following after the ship with his new pals. Won't be hard to spot a green and blue bird among all the white ones. I think the skipper's being optimistic, though. I think one of the crew, probably the Lascars, have captured Cato and boiled him. Lascars are well known to like the taste of parrot."

"Is that true?"

"I don't really know. It's just a theory." Timmons became confidential and gestured me to join him on the wing of the bridge, out of earshot from the helmsman, Patkul. "Speaking of mysteries," he said, "I saw our boy Ali this morning doing something interesting."

"Oh?"

"He was sitting on deck next to the lifeboats davits, all alone and reading. Oh ho, thought I. What can this mean? So I came up and asked him what was so fascinating, and he got rather sheepish and tried to hide the book. But I was too many for him and grabbed it away. For all I knew it was a manual on how to launch a lifeboat just before your ship blows up. What do you think it was?"

"*Othello?*"

"Eh? No. It was Edward Fitzgerald's translation of Omar Khayyam. The book that every schoolgirl keeps under her pillow to sigh over after lights out."

"Ah. That explains it."

"Does it? Well, then, good."

"It seems our friend is not what he pretends to be."

"Also good. I'm glad there's someone else aboard besides me. I pretend to be a public school man, when in fact no one would ever confuse

Llanabba with a proper public school. I am keenly aware of being an imposter."

"Next you'll be telling me you weren't expelled for drunkenness and fornication."

"Oh, no. That's all quite true. I wouldn't lie about something so important."

"Well, we'll have to keep a close eye on Mr. Ali. When you think of it, he makes a perfect agent."

"Yes. He's almost invisible to the naked eye."

And so the days passed. We saw no other ships and, thankfully, no signs of U boats—no sailors adrift on wreckage after having been sunk, no flotsam and jetsam or debris from a torpedoed freighter, no lonely lifeboats drifting. Even the weather was good. We didn't see any sign of the convoy, either, but we didn't expect to. The convoy would be taking wide course changes and zigzagging to confuse the enemy about its destination.

I had told the Fubars to keep an especially sharp watch on Ali. But so far he had done nothing out of the ordinary. He was still my helmsman during my bridge watches, and we chatted now and then in a friendly fashion. I learned a little more about his background and his life in Casablanca, but there was nothing remarkable or suspicious about any of it. I learned that his father had sold rugs. Well, of course he would have. I learned that his mother had a nasty temper and despite her innocence in matters of infidelity, she was difficult to live with in most other respects. A shrew? Apparently. I learned that Ali's own wife was modest and everything that a wife should be, and I saw a photo of her. She was indeed wearing a veil and an all-covering tent-like costume. She might have been any sort of bipod for all that I could see. Only her eyes peered out from her veil and headdress, and they were nothing to write quatrains about. But I made the appropriate noises.

"Very lovely," I said.

"Thank you, sir," said Ali.

And so the days passed. For all we knew, the *Carlota* was alone in the world.

On our thirteenth day out from Norfolk we were passing the same longitude as Madeira and only fifty or so miles north of it. In another day we would reach Point Ilsa, where we could expect to meet the convoy. It was November 6. It was getting close to noon and the three of us were on the bridge enjoying the day getting ready to take a sun line to establish our latitude. Flynn and Timmons and I were all feeling pretty much the same way. We were almost there. We were more than a little relieved, although we were aware the job wasn't done yet. But we also felt a sense of accomplishment. We had been given a difficult task, and it looked like we were just about to pull it off. We had been very lucky with the weather and very lucky with the ship's condition, for we had had no engine or rudder trouble and the *Carlota*'s ancient seams had not loosened more than usual and let in more seawater than was comfortable. Her bilge pumps were up to the task of keeping us afloat. So we were just on the verge of being able to take a deep breath and relax a little. Even Cato returned. It was not clear where he'd been. We certainly did not see him flying with the seagulls. Well, no one would have expected that.

"Damned bird has nine lives," said Flynn.

"Did he happen to mention where he's been?" said Timmons.

"Not a word. His lips are sealed, as usual."

"It's at times like these, when things seem to be going along well, that things happen," said Timmons. And of course that was exactly what we all were feeling. You know the old line in the adventure movies when someone says, "It's quiet, too quiet." Well, there's a reason that's such a cliché.

"It goes back to the Greeks," Timmons said. "Of course, most things do. But they went on and on about Nemesis. I assume you're familiar with the notion. It's a universal suspicion that when things are too good, it will attract the attention of the gods and one of them will toss a spanner into your works."

"Yes," said Flynn. "I'm told the Chinese mothers give their babies unpleasant names so that the jealous gods won't take a liking to them and snatch them to Chinese heaven, prematurely. I was told that one woman called her little boy the Chinese equivalent of Stinking Dumbass."

"How do you say that in Chinese?" said Timmons.

"I forget. Something that's very foreign sounding and difficult. It's possible of course that it's a fairy story or a joke. The man who told me was the same one who sold me Cato, so I've always been skeptical."

"An untrustworthy Chinaman?"

"The same."

"A tautology?"

"No, he was Mandarin. Lived with that white Russian woman who drank rum."

But nothing happened and we sailed along peacefully.

The next morning I had the four to eight watch. It was my favorite. For one thing Navy tradition was that the watch ended at 0715, so it was relatively short. Second, and more important, it was about 0600 when the mess cooks began to fire up the galley, and pretty soon the smell of fresh coffee and bacon frying and bread toasting began to waft up to the bridge, so that when you were finally relieved you were famished for breakfast and made short work of it in the wardroom, the officers' dining room. And finally, it is always a pleasure to watch the sun come up at sea. First the blackness goes to the darkest sort of gray that gradually begins to lighten so that you can begin to see the details of the ship and the texture of the sea, and then everything begins to change color and the sun comes up and, as Homer puts it, rosy-fingered dawn appears. On the other hand, you don't want too much rosiness; you know the old sailor's mantra—red skies in morning, sailors take warning. As in most things, balance and moderation are the keys. Thinking of Homer, I had to smile. Maybe it wasn't Homer who sang about dawn's rosy fingers; maybe it was some other guy with that name.

But I was only into the first thirty minutes of my watch when things started to happen. It was still pitch dark, and there was a pretty stiff breeze blowing. You could hear it making the rigging whine and moan, and there was a moderate sea, so that the ship was rolling and pitching and groaning more than usual. The big Swede, Olaf, had come on watch as the helmsman, saying that Ali was in the ship's sickbay.

"What's wrong with him?" I said.

Olaf shrugged.

"Not feeling good," he said.

The ship took a few sudden lurches and rolled a bit more than expected, and I bumped against the bulkhead by the door to the port wing. I heard some other banging, as if something had come loose from its moorings somewhere. Maybe in the cargo hold. Maybe on deck somewhere. A ship at sea is never quiet but you get used to the normal sounds of the ventilation and engines and the sounds of the sea and wind. They are continuous. But the sound of something banging against interior bulkheads, or even worse, against the outside of the hull, are immediately alarming. They shouldn't be happening.

Pancho and Lefty were on watch on the main deck, although I couldn't see them or much else for that matter. The moon was gone long ago and the stars were behind the clouds.

"Olaf," I said. "Let me take the wheel. Go down to the passenger cabins and wake up Otto and Reynolds, Smithers and Williams. Do you know where their cabins are?"

"Yes, sir. We play cards there."

"Good. Go tell them all to get dressed on the double and come to the bridge. I'll handle the wheel."

"Is there trouble?" he said.

"I don't know. Get moving."

Sailors are used to being woken at all hours, and most have essentially an on-off switch, meaning that they're able to be almost fully awake immediately, especially when there's an emergency. This wasn't an emergency yet, but the Fubars would know something was going on, and that would be enough to get them up and doing in a matter of seconds. They might not even bitch about it. Meanwhile, there were several more bangs, sharp and metallic sounding, as though heavy metal were swinging against the hull. And I was afraid that that was exactly what it was. But then it stopped. In one sense, that was even worse.

These damned undermanned merchant ships, I thought, as I gripped the wheel. It was moving left and right, a little like the wheel of a car on a rutted road. The moderate sea that was running made handling the wheel a little more trouble than usual. I cranked the engine order telegraph to change the speed from ahead standard to ahead slow. In calm seas I would have stopped, but we needed some forward motion on the ship to keep her nose into the seas that were acting up just a little. I tried to reach the speaking tube below the front windows so that I could call the captain, but I didn't want to let go of the wheel. So I just yelled for him. He was in his sea cabin just behind the pilot house. Skippers sleep like new parents with infants in a crib—never fully asleep, always half-consciously listening. The decent ones did, anyhow. And Flynn was certainly that. He appeared in his bathrobe a few moments later.

"What's the matter?"

"Nothing definite. But I heard some odd noises."

Just then the four Fubars arrived with Olaf, who took over the wheel. The Fubars were dressed and wearing their sidearms.

"Yes, sir?"

"I've been hearing some funny noises. Sounds like banging against the hull. Could be someone trying to lower a lifeboat. No word from Pancho and Lefty. Check it out. Use your flashlights. Your forty-five's loaded?"

"Yes, sir."

"All right. Split up two and two and check the main deck. We'll worry about the lower decks later."

"Aye, aye, sir."

They hustled down the ladder from the bridge wing, and I could see the lights from their flashlights spreading into two as one pair went down the port side and the other down the starboard. I thought about turning on the ship's lights, but I also knew we were damned close to waters where U boats could be lurking, and I wasn't sure that there was actually any trouble at all. No sense presenting a U boat with a gift target just because I heard some unusual noises. It could be nothing at all. But I didn't think so.

At that moment Timmons came into the pilot house.

"What's up?"

"Not sure. Could be nothing. Then again . . ."

At that point Reynolds came running up the starboard ladder to the pilot house.

"Starboard lifeboat's gone, sir!" he said. "No sign of Pancho and Lefty."

At that moment there was a horrendous explosion in the main cargo hold in the bow. The hatch covering of the forward hold blew up with a deafening blast, and a column of flame flew straight into the night air. Shards of the wooden hatch cover flew high into the air and then rained down on the ship and in the water on both sides of the ship. We stared for a moment, all of us shocked, our ears ringing, and we watched as the towering flame gradually subsided as though collapsing back upon itself and into a mushrooming cloud of smoke, but there were other flames now visible in the hold. The explosion had started fires there, and the odds were we were only a few seconds from eternity.

Timmons was the first to react. He sounded the ship's alarm, which was enough noise to wake the dead, and I thought ruefully it might need to in a moment. Pretty soon the crew scrambled out on the main deck, and Timmons went down and organized the firefighting party. The Fubars were first on the scene. They pulled the huge canvas-covered hoses from their storage reels, and when they were stretched out next to the now open hold where the fire was burning, they turned on the valves and charged the hoses and began trying to drown the flames, while those of us on the bridge watched and held our breath. The rest of the meager crew arrived and helped with the hoses and tried to clear away the burning fragments of the hatch cover. I saw one of the Lascars grab a burning shard with his bare hands and throw it overboard. Thick jets of water from four hoses were spewing into the hold as the men holding the brass nozzles struggled to keep the damned things from flying away. The water pressure was intense, as it needed to be. The light from the fire illuminated the men as they fought with the hoses. Sparks were flying upward and when the wind caught them they were blown back toward the ship's superstructure. The smell of burning wood and paint was noxious, and the smoke was billowing thicker now. And it looked like the proverbial scenes of hell, or the devil's blacksmith shop, for the firelight was dancing and flickering and throwing shadows, and it was the only light in the darkness. We could have switched on the ship's deck lights, because now there was no reason to worry about attracting U boats. The damage was done, or it soon would be once those flames reached the cans of aviation fuel and the pallets of bombs. But no one bothered. There was plenty of light from the fire.

Timmons was working heroically with the crew. They were doing all they could, and you could see that some of the crew at least had some experience with damage control methods. The Fubars, too, had all had some training at least in boot camp, so they understood firefighting at sea. Captain Flynn seemed to be in a state of shock as he watched the fire raging in the hold of a ship he had skippered so many years without unusual mishaps, beyond those you expect at sea. He was standing stock still and staring, or rather gaping, at the horrific scene below.

I told Olaf to keep her steady as she goes and ran down to the main deck to see if there was anything I could do. I relieved one of the Lascars on a hose nozzle and pointed the manic and evil genie at the base of the fire in the portside of the hold. The hose wanted to fly away, and it was an effort to hold it steady. The crewmen were also struggling with the other hoses, and unaccountably we seemed to be gaining on the fire. And also, unaccountably, the ship did not blow up. In the smoke we couldn't see whether parts of the fire had reached the gas cans, but it must have. Still, nothing happened. And as the frightful minutes passed we seemed to be getting the better of the fire. It was still raging and consuming the wooden cargo pallets and the paint on the bulkheads of the hold. But we were getting that under control, slowly but surely. Slowly the hold was filling up. There were several inches of water on the deck of the hold and some of the cargo was starting to float. Remarkably no one was shouting. Maybe everyone was holding his breath.

I looked over at Timmons. I was impressed by his coolness. He was managing a hose himself and at the same time giving orders to other men on the hoses. Absurdly, I thought that if he was going to be Lord Jim, he had missed his chance. I also wondered if there might be another bomb in another hold. If you wanted to make sure of blowing this ship to atoms, wouldn't you place bombs in all the holds? On the other hand, why bother? Why risk it? It would be risky enough to place one bomb and escape in a lifeboat, and surely one bomb would do it in a hold full of ammunition and gasoline. But so far it hadn't.

And it didn't. If it had, of course, I wouldn't be telling this story. It took us another thirty minutes or so to put out the last of the fire. A more modern ship would have had a sprinkler system that could have done most of the work. But *Carlota* had nothing like that. If the fire had been started in some of the lower spaces and smaller holds we may have been able to flood those and avert the danger. But this forward hold was nothing more than a boxlike hole in the ship just below the main deck and only two decks deep. It was perfect for what the saboteurs wanted to do, and they damned near pulled it off.

It was still a smoking, stinking hole in the ship when the last of the flames were out. The paint had been seared off the walls of the hold and the wooden cargo pallets were charred splinters. The gas cans were scattered everywhere, most were blown open by the initial bomb blast. Obviously, they weren't filled with fuel. There were no multi-colored patches of fuel floating on the water. The bombs, too, were scattered around the hold as though they had been dropped in there by a giant net from about twenty feet above.

I was standing next to Timmons as we looked down at the mess. The crew were still shooting jets of sea water into the hold so that more and more of the wreckage and cargo was floating. All the men including myself and Timmons had blackened faces from the soot and smoke. Timmons' white sweater was now charcoal gray and his jaunty white officer's cap was covered with grime.

"What the hell?" I said, looking down at the smoking hole that had been the hold.

"Yes, indeed."

"Why are we still here?"

"Why, indeed? Rather a good thing those cans had no petrol in them."

"What? Empty?" I thought by then that maybe they'd been filled with diesel fuel rather than Av gas. Diesel fuel is far less volatile. Although a bomb like the one here would surely have ignited it. Wouldn't it? "Empty?"

"Well not exactly. Fresh water."

"You knew?"

"Yes. I was responsible for loading the cargo, you remember. The bombs, too, are nothing at all. Fakes. The cans are quite useful, or at least they were before being blown apart. I think some might still be useable though."

"You knew?"

"To quote the redoubtable Molly Bloom—Yes."

"What the hell?"

"It's a long story, old chap. I suggest we make sure this fire is out for good and then have a cup of tea in the officer's dining room. I can explain it all then."

"The hell with tea. I have a half a pint of bourbon in my cabin. But we have something else to do, first—whoever did this got away in a lifeboat, and they may have killed two of my men. I want them."

"I do, too. And we'll get them. But really how far are they likely to get? The closest land is fifty miles away. Let them stew awhile. Think what they must be wondering and worrying about now that the dowdy *Carlota* has not blown up like something out of Wagner. Oops! *Quel cock-up*! When the sun comes up, we'll most likely be able to see them. And certainly they'll show up even on our decrepit radar. We'll get them all right. But let's muster the crew and find out who is missing."

"Is there much doubt?"

"I don't suppose there is. But measure twice, cut once."

When the fire was out, we gathered the crew on the main deck forward beside the blackened, stinking hole of a hold. Timmons and then the captain thanked the men for their work in saving the ship. The captain had recovered his composure somewhat, although he still seemed a little vague and distracted. Of course, there were two men missing—Ali and Patkul. Ali was not in sickbay.

Pancho and Lefty were also missing, and I was very much afraid we'd never find them. We might be able to learn what happened to them, though, once we caught up with the men in the lifeboat. And, as Timmons rightly said—we would.

Chapter Fourteen

"So are you really Nigel Timmons, first mate of the *Carlota*, disgraced son of a country vicar and well-known debaucher, seducer of barmaids, and ex-public school man? Or are you somehow related to an old Etonian named Bunny who is somehow related to the OSS?"

"Well, my name really is Nigel Timmons. And my father was a clergyman, although in his case he was a bishop. Very posh. But most of the rest of the story is my own invention. I always wanted to be an author, you see."

"And that school in Wales?"

"No such place. I was at Winchester, which as you may know, is very respectable. But from there I went to the naval college at Dartmouth. I'm one of you lads, you see. Lieutenant Timmons, RN, at your service."

"Does Captain Flynn know?"

"Up to a point, Lord Copper. Do you get the reference?"

"No."

"It's from one of my favorite novels, called *Scoop*, by Evelyn Waugh. Some of the characters work for a disagreeable boss named Lord Copper, who doesn't like to hear 'No,' so instead they say 'Up to a point, Lord Copper.' I don't know why this was a confidential mission, to be honest. But that's what they told me, and you know as well as I do that they are never wrong about anything and always have impeccable reasons for what they do and the orders they give."

"Of course."

"Have you read *Scoop*? Very funny. Evelyn Waugh wrote it. He's a man, by the way, poor chap. Who would give a son a woman's name? Turns out he married someone named Evelyn, too. Didn't last. Can't imagine why. But I got the name of my fictional school and headmaster from one of Waugh's earlier books. Did you catch that by the way?"

"Are you serious?"

"No, I didn't think you would. I'm not sure Waugh has caught on in America. Anyway, you asked if I was involved with the OSS and your friend Bunny. The answer there is—not really. He and the intelligence boys only came into the picture toward the end. You see, there was a time when everything about *Carlota's* mission was straightforward. We were going to be what we said we were—a merchant ship hired to the Allies to carry gas and bombs up the Sebou River in Morocco. And a company of Commandos. Your Navy was stretched very thin and the brass hats thought it was a good idea to have another professional naval officer on board, since the *Carlota's* civilian officers had buggered off—one to retrieve an erring wife, the other with a suspected case of U boat flu. So I was given the chance to volunteer. Now the interesting thing is *Carlota* is the sister ship of another banana boat named *Contessa*—exactly the same configuration and ownership. Originally, *Contessa* was supposed to be the backup in case *Carlota* had problems getting underway from Norfolk. Both are elderly old girls, so that was a legitimate worry. And because a shallow draft vessel is important to the mission, as I'm sure you know, it was prudent to have another vessel on hand."

"Yes. That much I do know."

"Well, about the time that we were scheduled for loading the intelligence boys got word of a possible sabotage plot. Your FBI people captured a group of four German agents who had been put ashore by a U boat on Long Island. Well, the coppers sweated the four Krauts and learned that they were part of a plot to blow up a highly volatile cargo ship that would be traveling with the convoy being assembled in Norfolk. The German agents didn't know where the convoy was heading. They didn't know it was an invasion fleet. They just assumed it was a fat prize that contained important ships of war that could be damaged by some huge explosion mid-convoy. That was to be coordinated with a wolf pack attack, but coordinated wolf pack attacks are easier said than done, because convoys have a way of eluding them in this world of visual contact."

"But a floating bomb mid-convoy is a sure thing."

"Right. Belt and suspenders, as you say. We say braces. Anyway, the FBI boys also sweated out that the target was the *Carlota*, so at the last minute the sensitive cargo was placed aboard the *Contessa*—she was berthed in Hampton while we were in Norfolk. We loaded some harmless looking bomb shapes and some pallets of gas cans and fifty gallon drums. They were filled with fresh water, so that they could be dried out and used later. Good thing, too, because when the cans and drums exploded, the water helped keep the fire down a little."

"I wonder why they sent me and my men. I suppose the plans were made and the orders cut before the switch happened."

"Exactly. You may remember that the French river pilot, Rene Thing-amajig, left just after you arrived."

"And he didn't know why he was being transferred."

"Right. And they sent him to the *Dorothy Dix* in case anyone was watching. He'll transfer to the *Contessa* once we get to Casablanca. And I might add that there's one of your Navy's lieutenants and a gang of sailors as the naval guard on *Contessa*. And there's one of me as well. The ship is a mirror image of *Carlota*, except that *Contessa* is carrying the real stuff."

"So the intelligence boys were on to Ali from the start?"

"Not really. They figured it was Patkul. He may have recruited Ali to help him, knowing that as a Moor he had a beef with the French—who, after all, are reported to be our allies, still."

"So they were on to Patkul."

"He was suspected, yes. I don't know how much you know about the Baltic countries."

"I know where they are, more or less."

"Well, no one really knows much more than that. But the traditional aristocracy of all those little countries has been German for centuries. The Russians have been sniffing around there, also for centuries, so there has always been tension there between groups—both ethnic and political tension. But the Germans are culturally ascendant. Patkul is named after an ancient German Baltic hero who fought against the Swedes. The Swedes were meddling in the Baltic countries, too. Patkul is as pure a German as they get, in Latvia. He's quite the swell in his country. Son of a count or something posh. Have you seen that Russian movie *Alexander Nevsky*?"

"As a matter of fact I have. The Teutonic knights are the villains."

"Yes, well, you'd expect that from a Russian. But it's accurate in the sense that the Russians and the Germans have been at each other's throats over the Baltics since the Flood. Still at it, of course. We knew nothing about the plot against the convoy, until your FBI caught those agents. Lucky for us. Otherwise . . ."

"Otherwise, we're carrying the cargo and we're toast."

"More or less. Lucky, eh?"

"What happened to the Germans, I wonder. The agents."

"Well, they let one off with life in prison for blowing the gaff, as we say, and after a brief military tribunal, they put the others one by one on a portable electric chair and pushed the On button. It's true. I never knew they had such things, and I wonder why they bother hauling one around. A bullet or a noose would be simpler. But I guess it creates the illusion of Yankee due process and justice. I wonder what that portable electric chair looks like. I suppose it could be nothing more than a kind of hotplate."

"How much did Captain Flynn know about all of this?"

"Not much. Need to know, old boy. Need to know."

"Which applied to me as well."

"Nothing personal. But after all, what purpose would it serve?"

"Might have saved me a few hours of worry."

"Yes. I understand. And I do agree with you about that. I should have trusted a brother officer. The captain, too, once we were underway. It would have done no harm. My mistake. I was following orders well past the point that was necessary. I do apologize."

"Fair enough. But I wonder why Patkul and Ali decided to do it here and now. Why not wait till we rejoined the convoy?"

"I'm guessing they didn't know we were going to rejoin. After all, the voyage is almost over. Madeira was their last chance to get away to a friendly or at least neutral port. If they'd have known we were going to rejoin, they might have waited and gone ahead with the original plan."

"That makes sense. Well, are you finished with your tea?"

"Yes. Although I must say it has an unusual taste. Reminds me of sourmash. I'll have to recommend it to my aunt. She's always interested in discovering new blends of tea."

"All right, then, let's go catch the bastards."

"Right. To adapt a line from Captain Flynn's favorite, Cole Porter— Let's do it. Let's catch a Lett."

"And a plagiarist poet."

It had been an hour since the explosion and fire, and during that time we had been steaming at all ahead slow, which for *Carlota* was five knots. Assuming Patkul and Ali were rowing in the opposite direction to get as far away as possible from the explosion before heading for Madeira, they were probably still well within radar range. Timmons and I went to the bridge and checked the screen. And there it was—a tiny green blip that showed up every time the curser passed over it. It was dead astern of us. With our binoculars on the wing of the bridge we could just make out the white spot on the horizon.

"I've been keeping an eye on them," said the captain. "They can't be more than seven miles astern. Are you gents ready to go retrieve them?"

"Yes, sir."

"Left full rudder!" bellowed Captain Flynn. "Come to course two seven zero. All ahead full."

Olaf repeated the order and spun the wheel and we started around to our reciprocal course. The old girl shuddered as we turned and as the engines added speed and we heeled over starboard. Full speed was fifteen knots, so we would be on them in less than thirty minutes.

I went back down to the main deck. The Fubars were gathered around the hold, making sure that the fires didn't start up again. A few of the crew men were still hosing down the sides of the hold. The water was about two feet deep and was sloshing around as *Carlota* continued her turn.

"Quite a party, eh Boss?" said Reynolds.

"You guys did great. Thanks for it."

"What the hell was in there, sir? We all thought it was gas and bombs."

"So did I. Turns out this ship is a decoy. The stuff in there was just harmless cans of water and some empty bomb lookalikes."

"It's a good thing."

"Yes."

"We going back to pick up that lifeboat, sir?" said Smithers.

"Yes, and the bastards in it. Any sign of Pancho and Lefty?"

"No, sir. I know damned well they're not in that lifeboat. We figure they got hit on the head and tossed over the side in the middle of the night, just before the bastards set the bomb."

"I'm afraid you're right. Go get your M1s, and bring me one, too."

"Aye, aye, sir."

A few minutes later we were standing on the starboard railing just below the empty davit where the lifeboat used to be. We were quickly closing the gap to the lifeboat and we could make out the two men in it. They had been rowing but had now given up.

"Do you know what mutiny, espionage, and piracy have in common, guys?"

"Yes—you get hung," said Otto.

"And do you know what Doom looks like?" I said, not waiting for an answer. "It looks like the bow of a rusted old merchant ship bearing down on you while you're sitting in a lifeboat with nowhere to go and no way to get there, and you don't know if that rusty old bucket is intending to plow straight through you or stop alongside and drop a grenade in your lap or maybe have the five guys with M1s who just lost two buddies open up on you. Five guys, eight thirty-caliber bullets each at a range of thirty feet. You don't know which of those things is going to happen, but you're pretty damned sure one of them is. So at this point your only hope is that the ship stops and throws you a line so that it can haul you aboard, throw you in irons, and take you back to civilization and hang you. And *that's* what you're hoping for. That's your best outcome. And that's what Doom looks like."

"Do you think the captain will ram them, sir?"

"I doubt it. He's a good company man. He'll want to recover the lifeboat. Well, it won't be long now. Load up."

We all shoved clips into the M1s and released the slides and waited, as we watched *Carlota* bearing down on the dingy white lifeboat. We could see Patkul standing there, legs apart and braced against the swells. Ali was sitting forlornly, one hand on a useless oar. I heard the captain yell "All Stop!" and the ship stopped shuddering from her unwanted speed and began to slide the last few hundred yards to the lifeboat.

"Man, there are some sorry-looking guys," said Smithers.

"And about to get even sorrier," said Reynolds.

The captain had judged his distance well, and we glided to a stop with the lifeboat a mere twenty yards off our beam.

Patkul was standing and facing us. He was doing his best imitation of defiance, or maybe it was real. Ali was trying to make himself as small as possible.

"Hey," said Williams. "Those guys are wearing Navy forty-fives and web belts."

"Bastards got 'em from Pancho and Lefty," said Otto. "And they've got their shotguns, too."

The captain and Timmons were on the wing of the bridge now.

"Don't try any funny business, men," said the captain. "We'll toss you a line and bring you alongside. We'll hitch up the boat and bring you aboard. The game's over."

Well, I guess Patkul's defiance wasn't an act after all, because he raised his fist in the air and then showed us two fingers and yelled.

"Fick dich!" Then he reached for the forty-five on his hip and started to raise it toward us.

"Fire!" I shouted.

We all started shooting simultaneously and the first of the shots slammed into Patkul's chest and lifted him into the air and threw him over the side, but the bullets kept coming and ricocheting off the old steel sides of the lifeboat and whanging off into the air. One or two of them must have hit Ali even though he was crouching in the stern sheets of the boat. He was partly shielded by the boat's hull. But only partly. He yelled out in pain and shouted something in Arabic that we didn't understand. Maybe it was "I surrender," or something along those lines, but we didn't pay any attention and kept shooting. The water around the boat was getting churned up by the bullets as we kept firing to where Patkul went over, but somehow Ali was able to avoid most of the direct shots. Suddenly, though, he succumbed to what I can only guess was pure panic, and he stood up and jumped overboard. We fired at his splash, too, and probably hit him more than a few times, although we couldn't see very well with the water churning up the way it was. Finally we all fired all eight rounds in each of our M1s, and the empty clips sprang from the rifles and clanged onto the deck alongside our empty brass.

I read somewhere that it took something like a hundred thousand cartridges to kill one enemy soldier. Maybe more. I forget. Some army bean counter with nothing better to do figured this out. We did a lot better than that.

I looked around the immediate surface of the sea to see if there were any ominous fins in the area. There weren't. But I figured there might be some pretty soon. There was plenty of blood in the water. Well, I wasn't worried about that. Those two were good and dead. And if by some miracle they were still just a little bit alive, well, I didn't care. Neither would the sharks.

"Why'd he go for his gun?" said Smithers. "There were five rifles pointing at him."

"I don't know," I said. "A Teutonic gesture, I suppose."

"Teutonic?" said Reynolds. "Is that another word for dumbass?"

"It can be. But I guess he knew he was toast, anyway. Wearing our guys' forty-fives was the clincher, and he knew it. He just decided to commit suicide. One thing is sure, we couldn't let him draw that forty-five. He might have gotten off a lucky shot."

"Suicide by Fubar. Bloody good," said Reynolds.

None of the men seemed shocked by the action. It was over very quickly, and besides all of them had been in a firefight not long ago in Cuba, when we cornered the crew of a damaged U boat. They had seen men get shot, had done the shooting, had buried enemy sailors on deserted beaches, had seen the devastating effects of our naval gunfire on an enemy ship and fueling station. They had seen the wreckage of torpedoed ships and some floating bodies. They were a little hardened to it all, even Smithers. And, personally, I was kind of surprised that I really didn't feel anything at all, didn't really give a damn. Later, when I had a chance to think about it, when the images of the fight came back, maybe in the middle of the night, I knew I still wouldn't give a damn. It wasn't full justice for Pancho and Lefty, but it would have to do.

We brought the lifeboat alongside and hosed it out. Then we attached it to the davit lines and raised it up and secured it. It had some jagged holes in the steel hull and more than a few dents from glancing bullets. The woodwork, the seats and the oars were all shot to pieces, and I could imagine Ali had a few ugly splinters in him to go with the bullet holes. But there was no damage to the boat that couldn't be repaired. You wouldn't want to use it before then, though. It wouldn't float for long.

We spent another hour or so slowly steaming around the area looking for any signs of Pancho and Lefty. We had to try. No one expected to find anything, though, and we didn't. And after a while the captain looked at me as if to ask if we'd done what needed to be done. They were my men; it was my call. I nodded sadly, the captain ordered the ship to come to course 090, and we headed back toward Point Ilsa. We would get there sometime late this afternoon.

"What about Pancho and Lefty?" said Reynolds. "Shouldn't we have some sort of ceremony or something?"

"I thought about that," I said. "I figure they'd like it better, if we waited till we got back to the *Nameless*. Better to have all their shipmates there to say so long, than to have it happen on this old bucket. It wasn't their ship. Ours either. What do you think?"

"Yes, sir. That fits better."

They all nodded, so that's the way it would happen.

"Why was that guy Patkul giving us Churchill's V for Victory sign, I wonder?" said Smithers. "Trying to make us think he was a friend?"

"V for Victory is when you show two fingers and the front of your hand," said Otto. "The European version of the bird is two fingers showing the back of your hand."

"So he was saying Fuck you?"

"Yep. That's what Fick Dich means."

"Does Churchill know the difference? Seems to me he goes both ways."

"Maybe. I'll say this for Patkul, he had guts," said Otto.

"Not anymore," said Reynolds. "They're splattered all over the boat."

"Funny," said Smithers. "They both seemed like such regular guys."

I thought about saying something like "that's who makes most wars," but it was too sappy, and I didn't believe it, anyway. I knew who started wars, and it wasn't the regular guys. It was the guys who looked like regular guys, but weren't. Guys with theories.

CHAPTER FIFTEEN

LATER THAT DAY, IN THE AFTERNOON, WE REACHED POINT ILSA. THE rest of the fleet was there preparing to split into the three attack groups that would hit the coast of Morocco simultaneously. It was a fine sight, the fleet, and we must have looked like a wizened maiden aunt at a debutante ball, as we plodded up, belching black smoke and carrying what must have seemed like a communicable disease—rust.

I didn't have any sympathy for the French, if they intended to resist our arrival. But I didn't envy them what they were about to receive, once those big guns on the battleships and cruisers and even destroyers let loose. Across the dark waters there were plenty of awesome shapes that surely would spell doom to the French, if they chose to be enemies, or welcome reinforcements, if they chose to be friends. Time would tell which it would be.

The *Nameless* was assigned to the Northern Attack Group, which consisted of the battleship *Texas* and the cruiser *Savannah*, and more than a dozen destroyers. There were also two aircraft carriers, both converted Esso tankers. One, the *Sangamon*, had her decks crammed with fighters and dive bombers of the kind that saved our bacon against the U boat. They would be in the air and soon sweeping French air resistance away and then turning attention to the troops and vehicles on the ground. The other carrier, the *Chenango*, was transporting seventy-six army P40s, the planes that would be based at the Port Lyautey airfield, once we captured it. There were ten or so auxiliary ships—troop transports and supply carriers and an oiler to service the group. And a few thousand yards away, keeping station on the edge of the convoy, was a ship that was the mirror image of *Carlota*. She was the *Contessa*—the shallow draft carrier of actual bombs and aviation gas, the ship was destined to ascend the Sebou River with Rene Malevergne as pilot.

We steamed around on the edges of the fleet and after a while spotted our destination, the *Nameless*, PC 475, amid the panoply of other warships. She looked like a gray whippet amid a kennel full of bulldogs and wolfhounds. She was doing anti-sub screening duty on the outside edges of the fleet. We came to within five hundred yards or so of her and signaled her with our light. In a few minutes, we could see her putting the whaleboat over the side and sending it our way. She was expecting us.

The Fubars and I gathered on the main deck of the *Carlota* with our gear and weapons. The whaleboat from the *Nameless* soon was alongside to pick us up. My orders telling me and the Fubars to return to our ship were part of the original package of orders I'd received—"*Rejoin PC 475 upon contact.*"

"Well, goodbye, Nigel," I said to Timmons.

"Goodbye, Riley. I hope you have forgiven me for the slight deception."

"Of course. You had your orders. I understand about that."

It had since occurred to me that, if he had let the secret of our cargo leak out to the crew, the fire and the loss of my men and the shootout at the lifeboat would almost certainly never have happened. Letting everyone know we were a decoy and that our cargo was harmless would have done absolutely no damage to the overall Torch mission, once we were at sea and under radio silence. Patkul and Ali would have stayed undercover. There would have been no need to blow up an empty, rusty bucket like *Carlota*, and no real way to do it. Maybe they would have gone on to acts of sabotage somewhere else, maybe on another ship in some future convoy. But there was no way to know about that, and all of us would have traded that possibility for the reality of having Pancho and Lefty still alive. But you couldn't really blame Nigel for keeping his secret, I suppose, and there was nothing to be done about it now.

"By the way," I said, "was there ever a Sally Free? Some fancier version, maybe? Daughter of a duke, maybe?"

"Up to a point, old boy. Sally was loosely based on a comely barmaid at a pub in Winchester. Her name was Rosie. Still is, I imagine. But she didn't get me tossed from school. She was much more discreet. And so was I. Next time you're in England, give me a call—you have my number—and we'll go out to Winchester and have a pint. Rosie pulls a very fine beer engine. And there's some really fine fishing nearby. We can have a day of Bass and trout. Ha, ha."

I knew about the fishing near Winchester. I had spent a couple of fine afternoons and even better evenings on the grassy banks of the Test River with Martha. We had fished there, in the afternoons.

"I'll make a point of it, Nigel. Goodbye, Captain," I said, shaking his hand and then saluting. "Thank you."

He had lost a few pounds during the voyage, but he still looked like Tweedledum in eyeglasses. Just a slimmer version.

"Not at all," he said, blinking at me. "And thank you. You and your men helped save the ship. The owners will be grateful. I'm still in shock about Patkul. He seemed like such a likable bloke."

"Yes, I suppose so."

"I'm very sorry about the men you lost."

"I am, too, Captain."

"Well, that's war, I'm afraid." He paused for a moment. "I don't suppose you'd like a parrot. Perhaps as a memento of our voyage? He's very quiet. He's like that old Prussian general who could be silent in six languages."

"No, sir. Thank you, but I'm sure Cato will be happier with your aunt in London. Please give my regards to Beatrice when you write to her."

"Who?"

"The lady in your photograph."

"Oh. Of course."

"She won't know who I am, but I feel that I know her, somehow."

In a very strange sense, that was true. The universal dream girl.

"Yes, I will be sure to do that," he said. "Well, goodbye, Lieutenant. Smooth sailing."

"Permission to leave the ship, sir," I said. This was the Navy's custom, but I didn't think it would hurt to flatter Captain Flynn with a little formality.

"Permission granted," said Flynn. And the five of us went down the companion ladder to the whaleboat, with me as the senior man, going last, as was proper. The coxswain greeted the Fubars with a friendly obscenity, and when I was aboard he put over the tiller, and we went dashing toward the *Nameless*.

What is it Dorothy says? There's no place like home? Well, true enough. But for a lot of sailors, home is their ship. Some have no real home except the ship. Others may have a place back on the land, some apartment in San Pedro or Portsmouth or San Diego or any number of Navy towns. Some may live in base housing. They may have wives and kids there, too. And when they're at sea, some may even miss those people back there. But a lot of them also breathe a sigh of relief when the ship clears the breakwater or the mouth of the harbor and falls in with the rhythm of the sea again—not so much because they're glad to get away, but because they're glad to be back. There's a difference. People are fond of quoting Robert Frost's poem about home being the place where they have to take you in. But for a sailor, the ship is a home where they don't have to take you and don't have to keep you, unless you want to be there enough to follow the rules and do your job. If you do, you're welcomed and appreciated, if a bit roughly, now and then. If not, they'll find a way to get rid of you. It's a comfortable feeling for a lot of guys, that familiar certainty—knowing that if anyone is screaming at you, it's not because you did something you didn't know was wrong; it's for screwing up things you knew you shouldn't screw up. It's all pretty clear, or at least as clear as it's going to get in human life. Everyone onboard knows the rules and believes in most of them, because most of them make sense, especially the ancient laws of seamanship and discipline. You're also allowed, and even expected to gripe about some of it. You're even allowed to think your immediate superior is a dickhead and that the food is lousy. But when you're being honest, you have to admit that dickheads are a fact of life in any kind of organization. And everywhere else. And the food is actually pretty good. Plus, there's no denying that the other guys onboard are your mates. Shipmates. Buddies. Contrary to sentimental opinion, though, they're not your family, which means they're not likely to disappoint you in any important way. Or you, them. You don't expect much from them except to be dependable when it matters. And you expect them to expect the same from you.

If you're a normal, average sailor, you don't think about any of this. It's just how it is. Uncomplicated. All of which is by way of saying we, meaning the Fubars and I, were happy to get back aboard PC 475, the good ship *Nameless*. Compared to the other ships in the fleet she wasn't very impressive—just 170 feet long with one three-inch gun forward and a pair of forties aft and some racks for depth charges. But she was clean and sleek, and she looked like a smaller version of a destroyer. And although she had a shallow draft and would roll in a parking lot puddle, you could learn to live with being tossed around like a cork in a wash cycle, and the bruises from being thrown against steel bulkheads would heal eventually. And she rode pretty smoothly in a calm sea—or so somebody once told me. Despite all that, she was a ship you could come to care for and eventually love, if you gave her the chance. There's no place like home.

Captain Ford was on the quarterdeck to greet us. He was smiling and was obviously glad to see us. He was dressed in his basic work khakis and had his properly salty skipper's hat covering his gray hair. But he was sporting brand new gold oak leaves on his collar. He'd been promoted to lieutenant commander while the *Nameless* was being repaired in Scotland. As most people know, the commanding officer of a ship is called captain regardless of his actual rank. Captain Ford was thin and wind-burned and red-faced and clear-eyed, and he was a welcome sight to all of us.

"Howdy, boys," he said, as we went alongside. We went aboard in proper fashion. The captain noticed there were two missing, and I had to tell him then and there that we had lost Pancho and Lefty to enemy action. The Fubars went below to stow their gear and check in with their shipmates, while I and the captain walked on main deck together and I told him how it all had happened, about the bomb and fire, and how the men did well fighting it.

"I'll write the letters to Pancho and Lefty's folks, sir," I said.

"Okay. I'm sorry about this. Truly sorry. But I'm sure they did their duty as best they could. Bastards ambushed them, sure as you're born. And at least you and the other boys didn't let the bastards get away with it. Well, we've got a job to do now, and there might be other casualties to come. Can't be helped. Wish it could. But it can't. By the way, they haven't sent us any new officers, so we're still shorthanded. Which means you're still the exec. Congratulations."

Once again I remembered Hemingway's idea that cowardice in combat came from not being able to control the imagination. I could see his point. Most men can't imagine being killed, because they can't imagine being dead, can't conceive of being nothing. So that doesn't really bother them too much. But they can imagine having their privates shot off or having disfiguring wounds or losing limbs or stepping on a landmine or being on the wrong end of a flame thrower. It's not something to dwell on, because it can be disabling, so Hemingway was probably right about that. But the dark side of the imagination also affects some ship captains in routine matters, not just combat. If you stop to think about it, there are so many things that can go wrong at sea, many of them things no one has control over, like the weather and human fallibility, that some captains burn up a lot of energy just thinking about them and thinking about what to do if and when they happened. To a certain extent that kind of contingency thinking is necessary. Contingency awareness is a Navy specialty, and after a while it becomes ingrained in you. But some skippers carry it a little too far and worry themselves into a frazzle, and that worry communicates itself to the crew. It makes the skipper touchy, which makes everyone on board just a little unhappier and more uncomfortable than they need to be.

Captain Tom Ford, aka "Model T" to the crew, was not that kind of skipper. Just the opposite, really. He knew the risks and responsibilities of command, but he didn't dwell on disasters that might never happen and probably wouldn't. Plus, he was a happy man. Being captain of a Navy ship was all he ever wanted, not because he had limited ambition, but because he believed that captain of a ship was the height of human ambition and achievement, and he looked down on any man who didn't understand that, and pitied any man who, through ignorance or moral failing, had wandered down another career path and spent his only life as a doctor or lawyer or anything else. He felt the way Mark Twain felt about a steamboat pilot—"*A pilot was the only unfettered and entirely independent human being that lived on earth.*" Well, that wasn't completely true of ship captains, of course, and it probably wasn't true of Mississippi riverboat pilots, either—except when both were underway. Everyone answers to someone, now and then. But it was as close to being the unvarnished truth as you're likely to get, especially when the ship has taken in all lines to the shore and has gone to sea.

There was another reason the captain was happy and comfortable in his role—he knew what he was doing. He had spent twenty years as an enlisted man, moving up the ranks, and when he was given his officer's commission before the war, there was very little about the operation of a Navy ship that he didn't know or at least have some experience with. And he knew the men; he had been one of them. They had no hope of running any bullshit past him, and they liked and admired him for that. He was in stark contrast to the skippers who suddenly find themselves in command before they know they're ready. Those are the skippers who are nervous. Captain Ford was never nervous, and if he had doubts about anything, he never showed it.

On mornings when I was on watch, Captain Ford would come into the pilot house with a cup of coffee. Usually this happened when the sun was just coming up and the sky was turning from black to gray and there were tinges of Homer's rosy dawn peering over the horizon. He'd sit down in his chair on the port side of the bridge, and he'd light his pipe, take a few satisfied puffs, and fill the pilot house with the sweet smell of tobacco smoke. Then he'd sip his coffee, and he'd smile and nod as if agreeing with something he'd just said to himself. He was the perfect image of a satisfied man. Those were the times, more often than not, he'd say to me, "Riley, there are people paying forty dollars a day to cruise around like this, and here we are getting paid to do it." And I'd smile back at him and say "Yes, sir," because there were times I felt pretty much the same way he did. Not always, of course, but sometimes.

But those relaxed and pleasant watches that smelled of coffee, pipe smoke, and a fresh westerly breeze would be on hold for a while, because later that day, in the evening, we were heading east with the Northern Attack Group. We were on our way to a battle.

As usual, we were part of the screen protecting the main body from U boats. I had the watch. The captain was in his chair on the port side of the pilot house, which was darkened, as were the other ships in the group. The three attack groups that had split at Point Ilsa were now steaming toward their separate targets on the coast of Morocco. Our group was heading for the city of Mehdia and the mouth of the Sebou River. The Center Attack Group would hit Casablanca just north of the city, and the Southern Group would land at Safi farther down the coast. At midnight we'd all be eight miles off the coast, and the transports would begin loading the assault craft. H hour was 0400. All three attacks were schedule to happen at the same time.

"One hell of a job of organization and seamanship," said Captain Ford. "The admiral and his staff did a fine job—getting all of us here where we're supposed to be, and all of us on time. To be honest with you, not many thought it could be done."

"Do you think the French will resist?" I said.

"Hard to figure what they're going to do," said the captain. "You'd think they'd welcome us with a song in their hearts and a kiss on each cheek. But most of the brass think they're going to fight, at least at the beginning. We have to assume they will. The betting is, the French will put on what they consider a respectable show and lose a respectable number of their troops and kill enough of ours to feel good about things. Then they'll quit."

"Doesn't make much sense, if they're planning to quit sooner or later."

"No, it doesn't. But there's always two sides to any story, and we only know our side of it. It's like those sad songs when someone's singing *I'm so blue cause you went away and left me, and why oh why did you do it?*"

Or, I thought—*what'll I do when you are far away . . .*

"But no one ever sings about the other side of things," he said. "Like how the one that took off feels. Chances are he's feeling pretty chipper. Glad to be out of it. Big relief. I expect you know something about that."

"I've read about such things, yes, sir."

"That a fact? Well, I know you like to read a lot."

"Yes, sir."

"Point is, we don't understand how the French see things, so we can't anticipate what they're going to do. Wouldn't be surprised if they don't know, either. They ain't famous for being unanimous."

"I heard DeGaulle said it was impossible to govern a country with two hundred and forty-two kinds of cheese."

"He would know, I suppose. Wonder if that includes Velveeta or Swiss."

"Probably not."

"Did you ever wonder whether the French make Swiss cheese? If they do, what do they call it? Can't call it Swiss."

"French cheese?"

"Could be. But I can't see myself going into a deli and ordering a ham and French on rye. Speaking of that, do you know that if you go into a Kosher deli in New York and order a ham and cheese sandwich, they'll make it for you, but they wouldn't be able to eat one, themselves. They can't mix meat and dairy."

"Yes, sir. I have heard that. Plus, they don't eat ham."

"So I've heard. You gotta admire that kind of sacrifice, seems to me. That's real piety, with handles. Going through life never having a cheese-burger, let alone ham and cheese? I don't think I could do it. Doesn't make any sense to me. One of the prophets in the Old Testament must have made a casual remark about it, and people picked it up and ran with it. They'll do that. It's what's known as human nature. You know, Mark Twain said God invented man because He was disappointed with the monkey."

"Yes, sir. I've heard that."

"But I think God invented man because He thought the sheep was too independent."

"Maybe the whole thing started when Noah cursed his son Ham, and people took it the wrong way."

"Noah did that, did he? I must have skipped that chapter. Well, Noah's sort of the unofficial patron saint of sailors who run aground, so it could be he did another dumbass thing and started this unnatural prejudice against a harmless sandwich."

"Could be. But I wonder—can an Old Testament Hebrew be a patron saint?"

"Why not? If a fella can do the job, I don't care about his religion. Take you, for example. You're a Presbyterian from Ohio by way of Hollywood, but I don't hold it against you."

"I'm glad to know that, Captain."

"Well, speaking of knowing, we'll know whether the French're gonna fight, soon enough. So far, they don't seem to have any idea that we're even here, let alone that we're coming for breakfast. Do you have your passport?"

"It's in my safe, sir." I assumed he was joking, and I guess he was, in a way.

"That's good, 'cause there's a chance you'll be going ashore."

Ah.

Chapter Sixteen

I SUPPOSE WORD HAD GOTTEN AROUND THAT I KNEW SOMETHING about the situation in Morocco. I didn't really, but give a dog a bad name, and he's likely to keep it. I had been there and I had driven down the coast from Tangier to Casablanca and then back up again, though that hardly qualifies as local knowledge or experience. And I did know some of our OSS people in country. But I didn't know if they would still be there once our troops landed, and I didn't know how my knowing them could do any good, anyway. If they had any sense, which they did, and if they had any knowledge of the coming invasion, which they must have, they would have cleared out and gone up to Spanish Morocco to wait until the dust cleared and the question of who was a friend and who was an enemy had been decided. On the other hand, maybe they'd stay on and start negotiating hard with the French so that the fight, if there was one, would be short and not too bloody. Either way, I couldn't see how my being there was at all useful. Well, the captain apparently knew something about it all, and he would tell me in his own good time.

Just before midnight Chief Warrant Officer Wheatley came to relieve me. I briefed him on the situation. We had not had any sonar contacts or seen any sign of the enemy, Axis or French, for that matter. It was pitch dark and all you could see was an occasional black shape in bare silhouette against the gloom—the ships in our group—and you could see the white wakes of the closest vessels.

The captain got up a little stiffly from his chair. He'd been on the bridge all day.

"I'm gonna lie down for a spell," he said. He didn't need to tell us to call him if anything happened. It was in his standing night orders, and besides we all knew what we were doing by this point. "We'll go to general quarters at 0400, unless we hear different."

"Aye, aye, sir," Wheatley and I said. "And I relieve you, sir," said Wheatley to me. I went below to my room.

The *Nameless* had received mail while the ship was in Scotland and just before she left for Operation Torch. The ship's yeoman had saved the letters that had come to me and had given them to me shortly after I came aboard, but I hadn't had time to read them yet. Or, rather, there hadn't been a few moments of privacy and quiet to read the one that smelled of Tabu perfume. Tired as I was, I decided to open that one.

Darling,

I'm in London now. I got the new assignment from Collier's and I'm excited to be here, though a little tired. I wonder where you are. Somewhere in the world. Are we star-crossed lovers, after all? No, I don't think so. We're past that stage. If I were on a balcony somewhere, I'd lower a ladder for you and we wouldn't care who found out about it or when morning came.

There are rumors all around town that something big is underway. I am trying to sweet talk every general and admiral I meet to try to find out what it is, but so far no one is talking. That is strange. I can usually wheedle information out of anyone with fewer than four stars, but so far no luck. Maybe I have lost my powers. Or maybe my charm batteries simply need recharging. Will you come to me and recharge them for me? I know you would, if you could. An hour or two on a blanket in the soft grass by the Test River would do it. Do you remember that evening? Of course you do. I sound like a schoolgirl, but I must say when I think of that time, I get a warm glow in places that would make the censor blush, if I got specific.

Please write to me when you can. I am so glad to be back in action, sort of, and I'd love to share some of that excitement with you. I am staying at the Dorchester. They still have room service and the sheets are Egyptian cotton.

Love,

Marty

Like I needed this. I should have left it unopened on my desk where its perfume would have added something nice to the atmosphere of my room without arousing too many thoughts and memories that were better left un-thought of, for the time being. Those kinds of thoughts were for mid-watches in the middle of the Atlantic, when there wasn't another ship within a hundred miles and the sea was calm. There were such nights, but tonight wasn't going to be one of them.

There was also a letter from my friend Hobey in Hollywood. I left it on the desk. I'd read it later. Right now I needed to sleep.

Blake, our only steward, woke me at 0345.

"Rise and shine, Mister Fitzhugh," he said.

"Son of a bitch," I said to the Universe. Having no sense of obligation, it ignored me, as usual. That is, unless it spoke through Blake. There were times when I thought that might be the case.

"I made some fresh cornbread," he said. Cornbread was his specialty. With enough butter spread on it, you could just about choke it down.

"Not right now, thank you, Blake. But bring me some coffee to the bridge. The captain will want some too, I'm sure."

"He's already up there, sir. Got his pipe fired up and he's on his second cup of coffee. He don't want no cornbread, neither."

"A triple negative, Blake. Well done."

"Thank you, sir."

"And it's a little early for cornbread, Blake. Don't take it personally."

"No, sir. I never do." In the dark I could see he was grinning. Well, that was not unusual. He was a happy man; he had found his métier.

I went up to the bridge. Chief Quartermaster Caruso was there. He was supposed to relieve Wheatley, but the captain was about to order General Quarters, and he would control the ship while the rest of us went to our assigned battle stations. He wanted to have a word with us first and brief us on the intelligence the admiral's staff had gathered about the coming operation. Some of it we already knew, but he was going to make sure we understood what was coming.

"Here's the situation, gents," he said. "The glow of lights you see on shore is from the town of Mehdia. It sits at the entrance of the Sebou River. There are two stone jetties sticking out from the mouth of the river, and they naturally channel the river water and create some turbulence as it hits the sea. Except at slack water, the tide runs pretty fast through there, going in or going out. Just beyond the jetties there's a shallow bar, and beyond that there's a boom across the mouth of the river. The boom's an inch and a half of wire cable with a wire net hanging below it. And to make matters even more interesting, there's an old Portuguese fort on the hill above to the right, going in. It's called the Kasbah, for some reason. Unfortunately, it ain't manned by old Portuguese. There's a detachment of French native troops in there and they have some artillery and machine guns pointing down on the river entrance and the first part of the passage upstream. They're packed in there peeping over the ramparts like Beau Geste and his brothers. There's also a few machine gun pits closer down to shore that can make things lively for anyone trying to cut that boom cable, and then on anyone trying to move up the river. After that there's twelve miles of tidal river that's got a sandy and muddy bottom, and at the end of the twelve miles there's a French airfield. The army's obliged to take it, so that the army planes from the Chenango will have a place to land, rearm, and refuel—and more importantly so that the French air force won't bother the landings and the attack as we move inland. I expect Navy planes from the *Sangamon* will give the airfield a good going over before the Army gets there, but it'll still need boots on the ground. It'll be no good to us if the Navy dive bombers ruin the runway.

"Any vessel entering the river will have to turn almost immediately north and run parallel the coastline for a couple of miles and then turn almost one-eighty back to the south. From that point on, the river looks like a bag of horseshit hanging from a fence rail. No doubt you've all seen such a thing at some point in your lives. If you haven't, then think of it as a U shape affair with the bottom of the U being the place the French put the airfield. The river's a quarter mile wide at its widest and narrower at the turns. The Army plans to make a kind of three-pronged attack on the airfield—first prong, knock out the Kasbah and then continue to the airfield along the south side of the river, second prong, head overland north of the river, and third, move up the river itself with a detachment of army Commandos aboard a ship." The skipper paused here and grinned slyly at the three of us. "Now I know you're probably thinking that we got the brass ring and the job of ferrying the Commandos. Well, we didn't. There's an old four piper destroyer called the *Dallas* that got the assignment. They cut down most of her superstructure to reduce her weight, so she'd draw less than normal, and there's a chance she'll be able to make it, once the army engineers cut the boom. Fact is, though, even if everything goes right, *Dallas* will still be dragging her old bottom most of the way upstream. The only other fly in the ointment is the French scuttled two old merchant ships right at the bend in the river where *Dallas* will make her turn south toward the airfield. They didn't do it by accident, so they must have figured something was coming their way that they didn't want. It will be a tight squeeze past those old buckets, and the flow of the water there suggests that it will be shallow, too. So, the whole upriver operation depends on a number of dicey factors, including the tide. Of course, it will be much better to go at high tide. That way we can go 'straight up the middle, Jimmy,' just like the Scottish lassies told us to. But the timing will be tricky, because getting over the bar and through the boom could slow things done considerably. Any questions so far?"

"I thought the idea was to take the *Contessa* upstream with the troops and the fuel and ammunition," I said. "The OSS snatched a French river pilot to guide her up to Port Lyautey." My brief adventure in Morocco had been part of the operation. I had been an unwitting decoy, or a duck as Rene said, but even so, I had some pride of authorship in the events. To see it all abandoned this way was annoying, even though I knew that military plans were generally written on water.

"Somebody changed their minds, I suppose," said the captain. "As of now the *Dallas* will take the Commandos, but your Frenchman will pilot the *Dallas*, so you can stop feeling like the girl who wasn't respected in the morning. Once the airfield's secure, he'll come back down and drive the *Contessa* up so that they can unload the ammo and fuel."

"That makes more sense, now that I think of it."

"The brass will be happy to hear you approve."

"It sounds like the trip up for the first time is going to be under fire most of the way. No sense sending a floating bomb in there, before the guns have been silenced and the French planes have been neutralized."

"Yep. The Army doesn't always have its head up its ass. Trouble is, the general in charge of this northern attack must have read too many novels about the Civil War bayonet charges. Doesn't trust the Navy gunfire to reduce the Kasbah to rubble and would rather take it by storm. Our folks think the *Texas* could turn that old fort to dust with a few salvos of fourteen inchers, but General Truscott is afraid our shells might fall on his own boys in the area or on civilians, which means we're dealing not only with the French troops, but also with the politics. After we kill a few of them and they kill a few of us, we'll want to kiss and make up and be friends again, so the less naval bombardment the better. You wouldn't want one of those fourteen inch shells to fall on the officers' whorehouse or their wine cellar."

"Any chance there's a little inter-service rivalry involved in this plan?" I said.

"Yep. Could be. This is the first rodeo for a lot of the Army boys, so they want to make sure they stay on the bull for eight seconds, at least. That way the reporters will say nice things in the papers, afterward. The worst thing from the Army point of view, aside from getting their asses kicked and sent home in boxes, would be for the Navy gunfire and airplanes to make the French quit before the Army had a chance to shoot anyone. They don't want to be seen standing by, holding our coats. Patton's in command of the whole shindig, and if you've heard anything about him, you know all you need to know. He's down south taking Casablanca, but his boy General Truscott's up here. They think alike. They both know if they screw the pooch here, they'll never again command anything bigger than a latrine detail."

"What's our job, then, Captain?" said Wheatley.

"Screen the transports. We'll operate with some of the destroyers. Some of the others will be doing gunfire support and guiding the landing craft into the point of departure for the assault boats. That will be about two miles off the beach. But we'll be hanging around the transports to make sure the U boats don't spoil the party. Lots of fat targets with those transports. Mighty tempting. Plus there's the French air force. There ain't many of them, but it doesn't take too many to cause problems."

"Funny," I said. "I was almost positive we'd be going up the river, either with the pilot and the Commandos or with the *Contessa*."

"You may turn out to be right after all," Ford said. "The Army's going to try to cut the boom this morning. If they can't get it done, there's a naval party standing by to try their luck. If they can cut the boom, the *Dallas* is going to start upstream, but if it gets too late and the tide starts ebbing too fast, or if they get hit by shore artillery and get disabled, or if they run aground on the bar and have to back out of the mud, or if they plain can't make it for any reason, we're next up. We're a lot smaller, obviously, but we don't draw as much, and we have just enough room for the Commandos, if they cuddle up next to each other nice and close. Most likely, that'll be tomorrow, if it happens. We'll know better after this morning. Anything else?"

"No, sir."

"All right. Pass the word for general quarters. No sense sounding the alarm. We're still trying to stay quiet. It's hard to believe but the French don't seem to know we're here yet. It'll get noisy soon enough once the assault boats start roaring around loading troops and heading for the beach. You figure somebody's got to be awake over there. But if not, they soon will be."

We had a front row seat for the morning's events. The assault craft were being put into the water and some were already alongside their transports, so that the Army boys could struggle down the rope ladders into the boats. Sadly, a few fell into the water and were drowned because their packs dragged them down, or they were crushed between the heavy landing craft and the hulls of the transports. Others would be drowned in the moderately heavy surf of the beaches, and I thought of the Duke of Wellington's remarks that the saddest thing next to a battle lost is a battle won, and yet for these poor guys there hadn't even been a battle—just the slip of a foot or the loss of a grip.

It didn't help that it was still dark when the assault boats began loading. There was only a moderate sea, but while that's comfortable for a full-sized Navy vessel, it will toss a landing craft up and down and side to side, and that makes the job of climbing down a rope ladder and landing in a gyrating deck all that much harder. Some assault boats that had been transported by amphibious units were drifting around trying the find the troop transports that they were assigned to. The darkness made the job that much harder. Most transports look pretty much the same even in good light. So there was a lot of engine revving and boat traffic going here and there and shouting. Although we were twelve miles out, it was impossible to believe that the French hadn't woken up by now.

They had. We learned that as soon as the first wave left the point of departure and headed for the beach. The French shore batteries opened up and suddenly it was the proverbial Fourth of July with tracer bullets flying our way and star shells illuminating the scene with their unnatural white light. And there were geysers of white water shooting into the air around the boats, geysers caused by French artillery shells. Our gunfire support ships opened up, and the din was ferocious. You could feel the concussion of the big guns from the *Texas* and the cruiser, *Savannah*. The generals had been wary of naval gunfire support for a number of reasons, but they had agreed on certain targets that were thought to be safe both from friendly fire accidents and from political repercussions. No whorehouses were in danger, nor any civilian neighborhoods. But French military installations were fair game and especially their artillery placements that were firing on our troops who were on their way in and on the troops that had already landed on the beach. Artillery from around the Kasbah was firing directly down the beaches where our troops were landing. Our counterbattery fire was effective, much to the probable surprise of Truscott and his staff, but there were enough French guns to make things lively and dangerous on the beach.

The beach itself was fast becoming a shambles of equipment and vehicles. The surf was pretty strong and the Navy coxswains handling the assault boats had their hands full trying to get to the beach and unload without broaching and, even worse, having to back out and turn around in the surf to go back for another load of troops waiting on the transports. Those landing craft are built to slide their flat bottoms onto a beach and deliver loads of men, equipment, and vehicles. They aren't built to handle heavy seas, whether inshore or farther out. Some coxswains couldn't do it and their boats were washed sideways on to the beach to join with some vehicles, jeeps, and a tank here and there that were stranded in the soft sand and mud of the beach. Most of the troops were under fire for the first time and were understandably looking to get off the beach as quickly as possible and were rushing for the cover of the shoreline trees and the dunes. That meant that some got detached from their units and were isolated and confused in the noise and darkness. Inevitably, because of the conditions and the dim light of predawn, and because neither the Army nor, frankly, the Navy was all that experienced in making large amphibious landings, some of the men were delivered to the wrong places. The guys who knew what they were doing in amphibious warfare were the Marines and the Pacific fleet, but they were far away now fighting the Japs, and most everyone here was new to the business. Someone would say much later that if we had been landing against a determined enemy, one who was well dug in and waiting, we would have been annihilated, so great was the confusion. And it was a sobering fact that there was just such an enemy, dug in and waiting for us in France. If the planners were learning anything from the first stages of Torch, they were learning that we were not even close to being ready to hit the beaches of Normandy or the South of France. Hell, we could figure that out just from watching the attack that first morning.

I was at my general quarters station at our three-inch gun. Williams, our first class gunners mate, was aft with the crew of the twin forty millimeters, and Bosun Wheatley was at the depth charge racks. I was connected to all of them and to the bridge by the sound-powered phones. I wished I had Williams sitting in the firing seat of the three inch, but he was needed at the forties. Otto was in the seat and Reynolds and Smithers were the loaders. Two other men were standing by to handle the shells coming up from the magazine. All of us were wearing bulky life jackets and steel helmets and our pants legs were rolled and stuffed in our socks. No one was sure exactly why we were supposed to do that, but it was standard procedure, so we did it. We were ready to load with variable frag ammunition—the stuff that was used against aircraft because it had a small radio device in the fuse that exploded the shell when it got near a plane. It was good ammunition, and it could be used against shore targets, too. Since it would explode in proximity of the target, we didn't have to hit something square on to do damage. We all knew that with the slow manual loading and the even slower manual aiming, we had almost no chance to fight off an airplane with the three-inch gun, but the forty millimeters aft would have a better chance, just because they were rapid firing and could throw up a volume of shells. So it was good that an experienced hand like Williams was in charge back there. We could deal with any French patrol craft or torpedo boats. If a U boat showed up we might switch to standard high explosive ammunition—HE. If we could see any targets ashore that were firing at us or any of the landing craft, we were allowed to take them on, too. But we weren't given any specific targets on shore to fire at. That was the business of the big boys, and they were sending naval gunfire liaison people ashore to act as spotters to identify targets and correct fire from the big guns.

So we spent the morning slowly doing figure eights on the outer edge of the transport area, listening for sonar contacts and watching for torpedo boats. We could see the Navy planes taking off from the *Sangamon* and heading inland to attack the French airbase at Port Lyautey. I remembered going past there when I was in Morocco before and remembered the barracks and hangers that were arranged around the airfield. I assumed our pilots were targeting those and also strafing any French planes that were parked on the runways.

Not that we had all that much time for being spectators. We kept up our figure eight patrols on the screen of the transports. We had no sonar contacts, but when the morning had fully arrived the French air force arrived with it. The first warning of this was a French fighter that appeared suddenly out of the morning haze and made a strafing run along the beach, scattering the troops who were also being harassed by artillery fire from the Kasbah. The French pilot came swooping down in fine fashion and fired machine guns from about three hundred feet and then took a steep climb out at the end of his run, and for a time it looked like things were going to get very hairy for the boys on the beach, because three more French planes followed in a line and repeated the action, and they made similar steep climbs to form up to make another run. Fortunately, at that moment fighters from the *Sangamon* showed up and there were some very fine looking dogfights, with enemy fighters and our planes swooping and diving and rolling and climbing, and you could see the puffs of machine gun fire trailing out behind our planes. The French pilots must have been inexperienced at this sort of combat, for one by one they sprouted trails of black smoke and plunged into the ground far behind the lines, so far that we couldn't see them explode when they hit. We didn't see any parachutes. There wasn't really time for the French pilots to bail out. They were hit quickly and went down even faster. One of the planes might have escaped and flown south or somewhere, but the beach strafing runs were over, at least for the time being.

As we were steaming outside the transports as part of our figure eight course, there came a shout over the sound-powered phone from the bridge—an enemy aircraft was bearing down on our starboard side. I could see something with the naked eye but when I used my glasses I could see it better. It was a French torpedo plane, an ancient-looking bi-plane with a massive anti-ship torpedo slung below its fuselage. The torpedo looked about the same as those ugly fish the U boat shot at us. The plane looked a lot like one of those British Swordfish torpedo planes that had damaged the German pocket battleship, *Bismarck*. Maybe the French had acquired a few Swordfish from the Brits. Or maybe it was the French version. So although it was slow and looked like a military antique, it could be dangerous. Certainly the sleek and ugly torpedo it carried was.

The plane seemed to be coming in at a leisurely pace. At that range and angle it hardly seemed to be moving at all, except it just kept getting gradually bigger. But the Frenchman wasn't really taking a casual approach; his plane was just old and slow and burdened by a heavy torpedo. I guessed he wasn't after us, but after one of the troop transports. There were eight transports anchored and unloading troops and arranged in formation. If he torpedoed any one of them, there'd be a sad

Thanksgiving for a lot of folks back home. No, the Frenchman wasn't after us, but we were in the way. That was a problem for both of us, but especially for him. Antiaircraft fire is always a difficult proposition, because the damned targets fly so fast that often the only way to shoot one down is to throw up a huge volume of flak and hope the bastard flies into one of the clouds of shrapnel and kills himself. Even with VT frag ammunition, you still have to shoot close enough to explode the stuff, and that was next to impossible with fast flying planes zooming past a manually aimed gun. The problem is relative motion, and if you've ever gone to the horse races and stood at the rail as the critters go thundering by, you may have wondered how the old cavalry men shot the Indians out of their saddles. The fact is, they didn't, very often; they only did that in the movies. In reality, the horses and riders were going by too fast to get anything but a lucky shot. That's why a smart officer would tell his men to shoot at the horses and hope the Indian aboard breaks his neck in the fall or that he's stunned momentarily and lies still long enough to put a bullet in him. An airplane that is flying parallel to you is many times more difficult to hit than a running horse. Truth is, it's impossible to hit with a swinging gun that's aimed manually, like our three inch gun. You can't possibly swing fast enough. But a torpedo bomber, because of the nature of its weapon, cannot use an airplane's natural advantage by whizzing past in impossible relative motion and speed. No, the torpedo bomber has to line up, usually perpendicular to the side of the ship he is targeting, and then come straight in to drop his torpedo. The torpedo, when dropped, will go straight forward in the direction the plane was flying. And the pilot has to drop it from just above the wave tops or it will bounce off course or even blow up. If the pilot's not flying low and straight at the target, the torpedo will miss. Simple as that. And if the plane is an old, slow bi-plane, a relic of interwar financial cutbacks and the belief that "all wars have ended so why invest in better technology," then the pilot of the plane is essentially flying a forlorn hope. So it was with the Frenchman.

"Otto! Target bearing 090 relative. Load!" Reynolds rammed a three-inch VT frag shell into the breech. Otto cranked the gun's bearing and elevation wheels and pointed at the target through his visual sights.

"Williams!" I yelled into the sound-powered phone, "You see that guy coming in?"

"Yes, sir! We're on him."

"Got him, Otto?"

"Yes, sir!"

We watched as the Frenchman gradually closed the range. He was a game one, that pilot. He could have dropped that torpedo well out from the targets and hoped for the best. After all, there were eight transports and the *Nameless* in the area; he might have hit one of them. But he didn't. He was trying to make sure. If it was a Swordfish, I vaguely remembered that his top speed was only about one hundred and thirty and the maximum range for the torpedo was fifteen hundred yards, which meant he probably wanted to get closer to a thousand yards before releasing the torpedo. The range of our guns was many times greater than that. So he kept coming. No doubt he was wondering what to do about the Patrol Craft "Nameless" that had crossed his line of attack. We were going slowly, so that our speed did not complicate the relative motion problem much, if at all.

I watched him coming straight for us. Maybe he planned to give us a burst of machine gun fire. Maybe he had one of those World War One nose-mounted machine guns that synchronized fire through the propeller. At that range I couldn't see. Maybe then he'd fly over us and dip down on the transports on the other side of us. But we'd never know, because at about twelve hundred yards, I figured he'd gotten close enough.

"Fire!"

I could hear the forties firing rapidly as the three-inch gun went off in a cloud of orange flame and gray smoke. And for a moment I couldn't see what if anything was happening. I got a good taste of cordite from the breeze that was slightly in our face.

"Reload! Fire!" More smoke, more flame, more concussion. Continued rapid firing from the forties.

Suddenly and shockingly, the French plane exploded in a huge ball of flame. Maybe we hit the torpedo, and maybe it was a contact fuse. Or maybe we hit the fuel tank. Maybe we hit both. In those few seconds Williams probably threw a dozen forty millimeter shells at him. We only fired the three-inch gun twice, and it was impossible to know which of the shells did the damage. Maybe more than one. And then I noticed that one of the destroyers in the area, maybe two thousand yards away, had also fired at the plane with their five-inch guns. But the plane was at an angle to them and presented a more difficult moving target. In relative terms, our target was hardly moving at all. He was just hanging there, getting bigger as he closed. So I figured it was our kill. That didn't matter tactically, but it would matter to the men and the *Nameless*.

In any event what had been a plane was now a ragged cloud of smoke and debris. And what had been a French pilot was now nothing at all. He had to have guts to come boring in the way he did, and it was very bad luck for him that we arrived in a position across his line of flight, just as he was more or less locked into his attacking course against the unarmed transports.

"Cease fire!" I yelled into the phones. And it was suddenly very quiet. At least, that's the way it seemed, because the ringing in our ears blocked any noise from the beach, or just about anywhere else.

"Jesus!" said Otto.

Martha's husband wrote a story called "The Short Happy Life of Francis Macomber." It was one of his better efforts. I thought of that now, as I watched the results of our shooting. That pilot had a very short life as a combat airman. I hoped he was experiencing some exhilaration as he came flying in, because now he and his antique airship were just a puff of ashes and scraps floating down from about three hundred feet. There were small white splashes scattered across the surface of the water. And then the bulk of the carcass splashed down and floated for a few seconds. But then it was gone, too. And the sea was smooth again, as though nothing had happened. It recovers quickly, the sea.

"Son of a bitch!" said Otto. "We actually hit him!"

"Yes. Good shooting, Otto. Well done, men."

So shocking it was to all of us that even Reynolds didn't have a smartass thing to say, except, "He came in just like a duck into decoys. What's the French word for duck?"

"*Canard*," I said.

"Well, scratch one *canard*," he said.

"I guess the story that the French wouldn't fight was horseshit," said Otto.

"Yes," I said. "Another *canard.*"

Chapter Seventeen

WE STAYED AT GENERAL QUARTERS THE REST OF THE DAYLIGHT HOURS and maintained our screen of the transports. They continued to offload troops and vehicles and supplies, and the beach kept getting more and more crowded with milling troops and milling vehicles, but gradually some of the units began moving inland to work toward their assigned objectives. The French air force didn't make many more attacks and the few that showed up did a quick one-eighty and went back to where they came from. This landing was nothing anyone would want to include in a textbook, except as a lesson in what can go wrong, but as the day went along, it was clear that we were making some progress.

The Army engineers assigned to cut the cable went in and were fired on by some heavy machine gun emplacements around the Kasbah. They took a number of casualties and decided to back off. Later that day a naval unit tried again and despite enemy gunfire managed to cut one end of the wire. Unfortunately, they cut the end that was just above the shallowest part of the river, the place where no ship could possibly pass, and they left intact the rest of the boom that still spanned the channel, which was the only way in, but which ran perilously close to the right-hand bank of the river.

Around noon we could see the *Dallas* cruising outside the jetties that marked the entrance to the river. It wasn't hard to recognize her, because all her masts and much of her superstructure had been removed. The tide had ebbed, and I was quite sure my erstwhile French friend Rene Malevergne was on board and telling the *Dallas* skipper that there was little or no chance to make it over the bar, until the tide changed. Nonetheless, they seemed to be getting ready to try it. Word had come from the Army that the Kasbah had been successfully stormed and that the fire from that quarter would be suppressed. It was a mistaken report, but the *Dallas* didn't know it. Then we could see the *Dallas* make her mind up, and she steamed at full speed toward the opening between the two jetties. She was obviously going to try to plow her way through the bar and then ram through the boom. Almost as soon as she turned to go in, artillery fire from the Kasbah opened up and sent huge splashes all around the *Dallas*. No doubt surprised, she prudently turned around and hurried back out to sea. There would be no upstream run today. It was just as well, because *Dallas* might well have run aground on the bar or been stymied by the boom and caught there, immobile, and a fine target for the gunners in the Kasbah who had not been taken by the army's assault. In fact, the army had tried the assault, had received a bloody nose, and pulled back. So much for cold steel.

When darkness arrived things settled down a bit, although of course you could hear small arms fire everywhere along the shoreline and a few miles inland. We didn't have much of an idea of how the Army was doing, but at least the situation offshore was pretty well under control. We secured from general quarters and set condition three, which meant we'd still man some of the guns, in this case the forties, but we let the rest of the crew get some chow and some sleep and there would be regular watches on the bridge and the engine room and for the lookouts.

At 1945 I went to the bridge to take the evening watch. It had been a long day, and things seemed to be quieting down a little, but we were still in the middle of an operation and the danger from U boats was still there, too. We were still screening the transports that were now unloading supplies and equipment and more vehicles. Most of the troops were on shore now, but they were limited to small arms. Much of the artillery and most of the tanks had not made it to the beach, yet. It was a problem with planning, again. Loading ships for an amphibious attack means thinking hard about the sequence of events and how the troops who go in first need to be supported by equipment, ammunition, and medical and food supplies. They will not need typewriters and pup tents in the first wave, but too often in the press of loading, the wrong things get loaded in the wrong ships and the right things get pushed in the back of the line so that they are landed last, rather than first.

The captain was on the bridge, still there after sixteen hours.

"Evening, Riley."

"Good evening, sir."

"You feeling alright?"

"Yes, sir. A little tired."

"We got our orders for tomorrow. We'll be going upriver."

"Instead of the *Dallas*?"

"Along with the *Dallas*. Staff thinks we're too small to break the cable, which is probably true. And the Commandos are still aboard *Dallas*, so the thinking is, we'll follow them in and provide some gunfire support if the Army hasn't knocked out the Kasbah by then. And since we draw less water, we'll take over if the *Dallas* runs aground and can't get off, somewhere along the way. If that happens, we'll take the Commandos on board and deliver them to the airfield. Might have to make a couple of trips. But without us, the Commandos could get stranded and shelled before they can get to their objective."

"Makes sense, I guess."

"I think so. But whether it does or it doesn't, that's what we're doing."

"So we tag along behind, like the little brother."

"Just like the little brother who wants to see the bare naked lady at the county fair." He smiled, as though remembering a happy day. "Ever see one?"

"I have seen a bare naked lady, sir, but not at the county fair."

"Well, you missed something. Next time you get a chance you should do it."

"Maybe I will. There's a good county fair in the part of Ohio where I grew up. Maybe I'll go back there one day for a visit."

"Something to look forward to. While you're at it you can look up your old high school girlfriend. She's probably tired of being married to that other fella by now and looking for some variety."

"That's a good idea, Skipper." And I had to admit, it was pretty good.

"Speaking of variety, I recall that the naked ladies at the county fair usually came in either the tattooed or the bearded variety. Very rarely did you get a combination. They tend to specialize. Like doctors. They generally have put on a few extra pounds over the years. You can't blame them for that—being around all that cotton candy and corn dogs all the time. That stuff all tastes good, but it's not what you'd call a healthy diet. The only greens available are the lime-colored snow cones. But even so, I remember the experience fondly. Yessir, for a ten-year-old boy, a fat naked lady is a mighty fine and interesting thing to see. And rare, too, since county fairs and carnivals generally only come around once a year, each, and the local town fat ladies are always dressed, when you see them on the street. Just as well."

"Did you follow a big brother into the tent?"

"No. I didn't have a brother. Had an older sister, but she wasn't interested, so I went in by myself. The barker said you had to be twenty-one to get in, but I lied about my age, and he took my nickel. He must have been pretty gullible, 'cause I was short for my age, and my voice hadn't changed."

"Did she have a beard?"

"No, she was one of the tattooed variety. She was so covered in tattoos you had to study her for a while to make sure she really was naked and you weren't getting cheated. Her name was Big Bertha, and the barker said the Germans named that cannon after her. I've often wondered whether that was true. Fact is, I've always had doubts."

He looked at me over his glasses.

"I suppose it's possible," I said.

"You do? Well, that's good to know. Eases my mind, some."

He stretched and yawned.

"You might want to get some sleep, Skipper," I said.

"Think I will. Tomorrow's likely to be a long day. The French don't seem ready to quit just yet. I was talking to the admiral's staff, and they said the Army had sent a couple of messengers in a jeep to try to talk sense into the French command. There was some thought about sending you because of your experience in Morocco, but the Army wanted the job and besides they felt they needed a more senior officer."

"I'm just as glad, sir. My experience didn't amount to much."

"I'm glad, too, because the jeep ran into a French roadblock, and they killed the colonel the Army sent and captured his aid, a major, and the driver. They took the prisoners to Port Lyautey. The major was able to send a message about what happened, but there's nobody in Lyautey to negotiate with."

"Not good."

"Nope. Turns out the major they got is a direct descendent of Alexander Hamilton. I suppose there's a historical point to be made there, but I'm too tired to see it. Anyway, we'll stay on screen duty until morning. Keep a sharp eye on the radar, and make sure the sonar operator is alert. I don't need to tell you that, but it makes me feel like I'm doing my job."

"I understand, sir."

Our radar screen was littered with blips. But they were all our ships. And I was glad to be out there among them and not in some cell in Port Lyautey. Or worse.

"Well, call me if there's a problem. High tide is at 0300 but we'll need at least some light to be able to see our way through the channel, so the plan is to go at 0600 and hope there's enough water to let the *Dallas* get over the bar."

"What if she runs aground and is stuck? Will there be enough water for us to go alongside and take off the Commandos?"

"The answer is, I don't know, but I think so. We'll have to see."

"I know a Hollywood producer who used to say 'We'll jump off that bridge when we come to it.'"

"That's about it. So we'll have reveille at 0500, general quarters at 0545. We won't need to man the depth charges for the run up the river. So have Bosun Wheatley split his men up to give you and Williams a hand with the guns."

"Aye, aye, sir."

"Oh, and Riley, that was good work with the torpedo plane. Well done. Tell the men I said so. I'll tell them myself when we get a moment, but it never hurts for a sailor to hear Well Done more than once."

"I will. Thank you, sir."

Nothing happened on my watch. We kept up our steaming up and down the edges of the transport formation. The sonar kept searching for a contact, but none came. Radar showed no new or unexplained blips. At 1145 Bosun Wheatley arrived to relieve me. I told him what the captain had told me and then went to my cabin and passed out.

At 0500 the word was passed over the ship's intercom—Reveille. Blake arrived about that time. I felt as if I had been stuffed in a canvas bag and beaten with a rubber hose.

"Rise and shine, Mr. Fitzhugh. There's fresh . . ."

"Goddamn it, Blake, if you say there's fresh cornbread, I'm going to bust you down to third class shit scraper."

"Oh, no, sir. I was going to say fresh coffee."

"Go away."

"Yes, sir."

I got dressed slowly and then went to our tiny wardroom to get some of that fresh coffee and then went up to the bridge. Captain Ford was already there. The morning was still dark, gradually turning gray, and the sea was fairly moderate. *Nameless* was rolling and pitching at about her usual rate—which was tolerable, if not strictly comfortable. We couldn't see much, but I knew from looking at our course that we were heading in toward the mouth of the Sebou.

Dawn didn't bother with her rosy fingers that morning. It just got gradually less gray and ahead of us about three miles, the *Dallas* was moving toward the river mouth. The stone jetties projecting from the entrance were visible, and the moderate surf was splashing against the jetty rocks. High tide had passed a couple of hours before, and you could see the turbulence that caused when the river water met the sea. On the cliff above the right side of the river going in, we could just barely make out the dark shape of the Kasbah. At that hour and that distance you wouldn't know what it was, unless you'd seen it in the daylight. But it looked all the more menacing for being so indistinct—Grendel's mother, crouching there.

A few thousand yards to our left as we headed in, I could see the familiar shape of the *Contessa*. She was steaming in big circles obviously waiting for the orders to enter the river, although I assumed the pilot, Rene Malevergne, was aboard the *Dallas* and that *Contessa* would have to wait until we had delivered the Commandos, before Rene could be brought back downriver to pilot the *Contessa* back up. Well, in any event, *Contessa* was apparently standing by to be ready for whatever came next.

"Signal from the *Dallas*, sir," came a voice from the signal bridge above. "'Good morning. Suggest you close up.'"

"Acknowledge," said the captain. "Signal 'Wilco.'" A message of "Wilco" meant it came directly from the commanding officer. "All ahead full," said the captain.

It wasn't my watch and we would be going to general quarters in a few minutes, so I was just curious if there had been any changes since last night. But there weren't, and I could feel the surge of our engines as we revved up to full speed, which would be about twenty-two knots. *Nameless* shuddered, as she always did at that speed, until she had a chance to get adjusted.

"Sound general quarters," said the captain, and the bosun's mate of the watch passed the word and sounded the alarm. The *dong dong dong* of the alarm was followed by the announcement, "General quarters, general quarters, all hands man your battle stations." That was always enough to send a thrill through you—not a thrill of pleasure, either. But certainly one of excitement. There wasn't any reason for silence now.

I went down to my station by the three-inch gun and put on the sound-powered phones. The gun crew came running in their life jackets and helmets and took their stations by the gun. Otto in the firing seat, Reynolds and Smithers standing by to load. I put on my life jacket and helmet. In a few minutes I heard Williams saying, "After mount manned and ready, sir." So I reported to the bridge that all weapons were manned and ready, and we watched in silence as we closed the gap between us and the *Dallas*. She was just about to enter the channel between the two jetties.

That's when the guns from the Kasbah opened up. The *Dallas* was through the jetty and she was making a sharp turn to the right to pick up the deepest water of the channel. You could see her hugging the stone banks, and it was a good thing Rene was aboard because no skipper without his local knowledge would have gone so close to the right bank. But that's where the channel was. Not surprisingly, the French had removed the channel markings when they strung the boom.

I had my binoculars focused on the *Dallas*. There were huge blossoms of white water two at a time as shells hit the water and detonated. They were straddling *Dallas*—never a good sign for the target. Other shells landed on beach near the jetty and blasted sand and rocks sky high. But *Dallas* kept going. Soon she was through the jetty and approaching the bar. Now we'll see, I thought. We had closed up to within five hundred yards of *Dallas* and were just outside the jetties. So far the Kasbah hadn't bothered with us. Maybe they were thinking that if they hit and stranded the *Dallas* they would effectively block the channel for good—or for at least the duration of the whole attack. And if they were thinking that, they were right.

Dallas powered on—until she hit the bar. Then she stopped. If she had had any masts they would have toppled over from the sudden shock of running head-on into the mud of the bar. For a few moments *Dallas* was immobile, and the shells from the Kasbah kept coming. Their gunners were efficient loading and firing, but they weren't very good shots. The blossoms of white water and mud and sand kept appearing all around *Dallas*, but she wasn't hit. Not yet. She shuddered a little as she started to back down. She was going to back up and give herself a little room and then crank up to flank speed and hit that bar again. There was no choice in the matter by this point. The *Nameless* crept forward to be ready to follow *Dallas*, if she broke through. It wouldn't be hard to see her course. We'd just follow her wake of muddy water. *Dallas* backed off a couple hundred yards from the bar, and then I could see her stern dip as she put her foot to the floor, and the water boiled up from her props and she steamed forward with real purpose and hit the bar again. It was a solid blow, and she staggered and slowed almost to a stop. Almost. But her props were still churning at flank speed RPM even though she was only barely moving forward. I didn't know much about engineering, having been a deck officer all the time I was in the Navy—and glad of it—but I was pretty sure there were officers and petty officers in the engine room who were watching dials and sweating and worrying desperately about bearings overheating and other such arcane matters, so beloved of the snipes, aka, engineers. But *Dallas* was moving. She was creeping forward, sending back clouds of sand and river bottom, like a truck spinning its tires in the mud. But she wasn't completely stuck. She ground forward like someone pushing a piano across a heavy carpet—straining, but making some progress, afraid to stop for fear of losing what little momentum and forward thrust she had. The seconds went by and the shells kept falling all around, but none of them hit either one of us. It was hard to believe. You'd have thought that they might land just one out of sheer luck. But they didn't. And *Dallas* kept pushing, straining her engines and inching forward. Then suddenly she was through and beyond the bar, and she shot into the clear deeper water with her engines still revving flank speed, and then she cut her speed for fear of crashing into the bank like a car out of control. I could hear her crew giving a cheer. Then I could feel our engines revving up, and we headed for the jetty and shot through it and turned hard right to follow in *Dallas*'s path, and we could see the trail of mud in the water and we slid through the bar only grazing the bottom on our port side, at which point the gunners in the Kasbah noticed us and threw a couple shells our way. They missed badly, but we were in the battle now. We could see the flashes of the guns around the fort and just then a machine gun opened up from the slope just below the walls of the fort. The bastard was aiming at us.

"Load!" I shouted. "After mount. You see that machine gun?"

"Yes, sir!"

"Shoot the bastards! Fire at will!"

"Aye, aye, sir!"

"Reynolds, load HE."

Reynolds slammed a shell into the three-inch and Otto swung the gun around to point at the machine gun. It was pretty much point blank range. For us. But for him, too, I realized.

The three-inch gun went off once, twice, three times, as the men reloaded efficiently, and I could see the explosions of dirt around the machine gun emplacement on the hillside. After the third shot one of the French troops decided he'd had enough. He stood up and started running up the hill, but the others stayed at it, and between our shots I could hear the pinging of machine gun bullets hitting our hull. I could see the shells from the forties pounding all around that machine gun, but the French were pretty well dug in and kept on firing. Then we fired another three-inch round, and suddenly the machine gun position exploded in a brilliant white flash and dense white smoke. Plumes of ostrich feather smoke and burning debris shot into the sky hesitated and then arced back down and fell into the river and all around the French.

"What the hell?" I said.

"Christ! Willy Peter," said Reynolds. "I guess one got mixed in with the HE."

Willy Peter. White phosphorous. The worst sort of shell to get sent your way, because it started a fire that could not be extinguished. The stuff even burned under water, and pity the man who got hit with it. It would burn until it used itself up, usually well after it had burned through the flesh it hit. Usually, it was used to mark targets, because the white smoke was so bright and dense and the fire it started blazed out of control and made a fine torch. Now and then it was used against live targets. There was some talk about the morality of using it against people. There'd be more talk as the war went on. But no one stopped using it.

The white smoke didn't blow away for a minute or so, but when it did, it was clear the machine gun and its handlers were gone. There was a big hole where they had been, and the hole was dusted over with white residue. It was still smoking a little. The smoke looked like morning ground fog, but it wasn't.

The shells from the Kasbah were still coming now and then, and I realized that *Dallas* was also firing her three-inch guns at the walls of the fort and at the artillery emplacements along the hillside. The Commandos were lined up and crouching on the port side of *Dallas*, out of the sight of the enemy gunners. I wondered if their weight might cause *Dallas* to list slightly and make her upstream movement all that more perilous. But there wasn't any way to arrange them evenly, because on the starboard side they'd be in plain sight of the enemy machine guns and artillery.

And suddenly dive bombers from the *Sangamon* arrived and started pounding the fort. Either Captain Ford or the *Dallas* skipper had radioed for air support. The Kasbah was a big target and hard to miss, and they didn't. A couple of Wildcat fighters showed up, too, and strafed the artillery positions around the fort. I wondered about the morale of the French troops. A lot of them were natives, and they must have begun wondering why they were enduring this storm of fire on behalf of some faraway foreign politicians. And if Beau Geste and his brothers were up there with the Foreign Legion, I was pretty sure they were having doubts, too.

Up ahead the *Dallas* was approaching the boom. Once again she gathered herself and then went all ahead flank straight into the inch and a half wire and the wire net hanging below it. I could hear the grinding sound from where we were, because we had moved up even closer and were only a hundred yards or so behind. *Dallas* shuddered and paused for a moment as she hit, but then she surged forward and broke through the boom. We could see the floats that had held the boom drift away to the right and left and we raised a cheer in response to the cheer from the *Dallas*, and we followed her through the gap. Now we were both into the river proper, headed north toward the hairpin turn that would take us back to the south, toward the airfield.

Chapter Eighteen

That northernmost stretch of the river actually straightened out to the east for about three thousand yards before turning south. We steamed along behind the *Dallas* without too much trouble. Now and then snipers would fire at us, but no one on *Nameless* was hit, and I think *Dallas* made it through unharmed, too. I wondered again about the motivation and morale of the French troops. Give a soldier—or a sailor—a weapon and teach him how to use it, and at some point he'll want to fire it. That doesn't mean he's all that aggressive or motivated to kill someone, especially if that someone isn't shooting at him. A large ship steaming up the river makes an attractive target that seems like a wholly un-human thing to shoot at, like a boy plinking cans with a twenty-two. And a ship's hard to miss. A soldier who isn't very motivated can fire off a few rounds at a ship going by and then tell his grandkids he was in a battle.

Just at the end of this eastward reach were the two scuttled French merchantmen. The enemy did a pretty good job of placing them across our only line of approach, but they left just enough room for us to squeeze by. The morning was moving along, which meant the tide was ebbing and the current through the gap between those two old rusted buckets was pretty strong and would require both of us, *Dallas* and *Nameless*, to shoot the gap under almost full power, and then, once through, to make a sharp turn to the right to head south. If we couldn't make the turn in time, the power we needed to get through the gap could shoot us into the far bank of the river. A ship actually slides through the water as it turns, as though it's skidding in the snow. It does not follow a line, like a vehicle on a dry road. And so even if we ordered right full rudder just after going through the gap, there was a danger of sliding into the far bank. It was a delicate maneuver, especially for the larger *Dallas*. And there was no time to waste because of the tide going out. We needed to get the Commandos ashore and then get out of there before we both ran aground. I figured *Nameless* was pretty sure to make it, because of our shallower draft. But *Dallas* was another story.

Once again the *Dallas* went ahead full, and she shot straight for the gap between the merchants. She rolled a bit, once to starboard and once to port, and I assume she touched bottom then, but she shot through the gap in fine style and made her turn to the right very smartly and headed upstream toward the airfield, which was about two thousand yards away and in sight on the right bank. Along the right bank we could see some of our troops. They were supposed to be moving toward the airfield, too. They waved, but they were dug in because of some French artillery or machine gun installations in their way. I figured they weren't waving out of friendliness, but maybe to let us know a few well aimed shots at the French would be welcome.

Nameless surged toward the gap and slid through with no trouble and made the turn in *Dallas*'s wake, and while *Dallas* kept going at full speed, we slowed down. Captain Ford must have had some kind of premonition, because we were letting the *Dallas* put some distance between us. When she was about a thousand yards ahead and almost abaft the airfield, she rammed into a mud bank and was hard aground. I could imagine the men on the bridge almost being thrown through the front windows. The ebbing tide and a shifting river bottom had combined to stop her dead in her tracks. Rene knew about the tide, but he'd been away from the river for quite a while, and this new mud bank or shoal was a surprise. *Dallas* going in there at top speed was a calculated risk, because she wanted to get the commandos ashore and get out of there while the ebbing tide left her enough water. But the gamble didn't work. And the fact that she was going full speed ahead meant that when she hit the mud bank, her momentum carried her deep into it. For several minutes she tried reversing her engines to slide out of that mud trough she'd made, but it was no good. She churned up a lot of thick muddy water, but she was stuck, until someone could tow her off or until the tide came in and lifted her up and let her back out, finally. Maybe it would take both a tow and the tide.

Bosun Wheatley came running forward to where I was standing. He had two of his deck hands with him.

"We got our orders from *Dallas*. Skipper's going to go alongside and take off the Commandos," he said.

"Is there enough water for us?"

"Appears to be. We'll tie up on their portside, take off the Commandos, and then run them into shore. We can get close enough to run a couple of gangways at least to the shallow water. They might get their feet wet, but that's okay."

"Makes you wonder how in the hell they were supposed to get off *Dallas* in the first place."

"Rubber boats. They still got 'em, but their skipper thinks it'll be faster and safer if we take them in. That way they'll all land at once and not in dribs and drabs in a few rubber boats making trips back and forth."

"Makes sense, I guess."

"Once we get them ashore, we'll come back and rig a tow line to *Dallas*'s stern and see if we can pull her off. If we can't, we're ordered to take the Frenchman back down the river and deliver him to the *Contessa*, so he can bring her in whenever the river rises enough."

"How about *Dallas*? She's a sitting duck."

"Worse than that. She's a sitting decoy. A duck can at least fly off. If we can't pull her off, she'll have to wait for a tug or the tide. But there doesn't seem to be much enemy activity around the airfield. There's some artillery just ahead on the right bank. It's in a kind of redoubt, and we've been asked to deal with it before we go alongside *Dallas*. That way those Army boys on shore can move forward to the airfield at the same time we land the Commandos. Maybe the French will do the smart thing and leave. Could be they already have. The Navy planes worked it over pretty good. I'm kind of surprised they didn't nail that redoubt. Well, I've got to get the lines ready for going alongside, but the skipper said for you to see if you can take out that French artillery."

So we started forward toward the *Dallas*. When we were still a few hundred yards astern of her we could see the French artillery emplacement that was pinning down the Army on the right bank. There were two guns and a couple of mortars as well as a heavy machine gun, all arranged in a well-prepared redoubt. But it wasn't made of concrete. The guns were placed behind low earthen walls. The French had obviously figured someone would be coming for the airfield along this bank of the river. For some reason they hadn't counted on getting fire from a ship sailing immediately to the side. I suppose they were figuring the bar and the boom would prevent any enemy from coming upriver, so they only prepared for an overland assault. Their guns were positioned to fire down the bank and into the mouth of the river, but not to the side. I figured the range was about a thousand yards. I could see the French pretty clearly and see the muzzles of their guns.

"Otto! Target bearing 090 relative."

He swung the gun around to that bearing.

"Do you see that redoubt?"

"No, sir."

"Here. Use my binoculars."

"One of these days," said Reynolds, "when we grow up, they'll give us a radar system that can find the target and point the gun. This way we're doing it the Chinese way."

"I see them," said Otto, handing back my glasses.

"Well, then let's see if we can ruin their day. Load HE."

"Not Willy Peter, by accident, sir?" said Reynolds. "You want to ruin their day, that'll do it."

"HE."

"Praise the Ford and pass the ammunition," said Reynolds. He slammed a shell into the breach. Otto made a few manual adjustments as he squinted through the sight.

The three-inch fifty naval gun is a very fine, flat shooting, accurate gun that has a range of up to thirteen thousand yards. So we were once again at point blank range. The French redoubt was on a level plain. There were no trees between us, no hills or hillocks. Nothing but some marshy ground. The only thing between us and the target was a few cattails. There were some trees in the back and on the side of the redoubt. But there weren't any in our line of sight. The trees looked like cottonwoods, but I couldn't be sure of that. They were fairly tall and thick and leafless.

"Got 'em, sir," said Otto.

"Fire!"

Once again there came a deafening boom and a brilliant flash of orange followed by the dense gray smoke. I watched through my binoculars to see the fall of shot. It must have whistled directly over the heads of the French gunners, because it hit one of those cottonwoods and blew it to splinters. I could see the French gunners diving for cover.

"Reload! Fire!"

The *Nameless* must have rolled to starboard slightly at that moment because the next shot hit the mound of dirt surrounding the redoubt, and it sent up a very fine explosion of dirt and rocks and showered the French gunners with debris.

"Reload. Fire!"

We were back on an even keel and the third shot hit another tree and blew the trunk into flying shards. The big branches toppled over in slow motion and fell into the redoubt. And at that point the French gunners had enough, and I could see them climbing over the walls of the redoubt and running off in all directions away from the river. At the same time, the Army boys who had been pinned down raised a shout and charged forward in fine style. They even had fixed bayonets. Somewhere, Lee and Grant were smiling. In a few minutes, our troops were at the redoubt and in possession. From there it would be an open field ahead to the airport, and it would be a race between them and our Commandos as to who would get there first.

"Those Frenchies wouldn't be running if we'd hit them with Willy Peter," said Reynolds.

"I know," I said. I didn't have anything against trying to kill the enemy. They were, after all, trying to kill us. But I didn't much want to do it that way.

"They'd be crispy French fries. French toast. Ha! French toast! Get it?"

I thought about telling Reynolds that obvious jokes usually don't get a laugh. But I didn't.

"Good shooting, Otto," I said.

"Wow!" said Smithers. "This gun might be kind of basic, but it sure shoots straight."

"Straight up the middle, Jimmy," said Reynolds.

We moved slowly to close the distance between us and the *Dallas*, and as we slid alongside Bosun Wheatley and his deck handlers tossed lines to the *Dallas* crew to tie us up. There was a height difference, but *Dallas* had rigged some rope nets to let the Commandos come aboard. They were carrying their rifles and backpacks but not much else. If they ran into any heavy opposition, they'd be severely outgunned. But I guess that's another reason we were there—fire support.

"Welcome aboard, men!" said Captain Ford from the wing of the bridge. "The tour today will take roughly five minutes, and no food or beverages will be served."

The men cheered and waved and arranged themselves all around the main deck on both sides of the ship. They were a rough-looking bunch, and I began to rethink what I had thought about some soldiers not especially wanting to shoot anyone.

The skipper of the *Dallas* who was on his bridge wing watched the operation, and when all the men were on board we took in the lines and started forward.

"We'll be back shortly, Bob, and try to pull you off," said Captain Ford to the *Dallas*'s skipper.

It really did take only five minutes to get the men ashore. We pulled as close as possible to the bank. We could feel the starboard side of the hull brush against the mud of the riverbank, and the deck gang ran a gangway over the side from the quarterdeck. We were close enough so that the other end of the gangway was on dry land. The Commandos gave a whoop and ran on to shore and spread out in very fine style and headed for the airfield in double time. There was no firing and in only a few moments we could see the Commandos linking up with the troops coming up along the right bank, and it looked as though the airfield would be ours without a shot being fired.

"The Frenchies took off, looks like," said Otto.

Just then a shell landed fifty yards off the portside of the *Dallas*. It exploded and sent a shower of water and mud over the *Dallas*'s fantail and depth charge racks.

"Not all of them!" said Smithers.

The firing seemed to be coming from dead ahead. The *Dallas*'s forward gun crew was loading and firing straight up the river toward the town of Port Lyautey, which was about a mile and a half away and in full sight. More shells came our way and we could see the flashes of the French guns.

"Join the party, Riley," came the order from the bridge. So we loaded another high explosive round and Otto pointed in the general direction of the French battery, and we fired a half dozen rounds toward the city, while *Dallas* did the same. We got off those six rounds in under a minute. I could see our shells hitting and exploding randomly and we probably blew up some warehouses or taverns. While we were shooting, a couple of Wildcats showed up and strafed the area, and a Dauntless dive bomber dropped something on them. I couldn't tell if we hit their guns; there was too much smoke from our shells and from the bomb and strafing. But I think we came close enough to discourage them. Anyway, they quit, and then, after firing a few more souvenirs at them, we did, too.

We backed away from the riverbank and steamed slowly forward and crossed the bow of the *Dallas* and then went around behind so that we were stern to stern. We passed her a line. Her deck crew pulled it in. Tied to the end of line was a manila towing cable. *Dallas* hauled the cable in and secured it. We moved forward slowly about fifty yards, paying out the cable as we went. Then we stopped for a moment, and Bosun Wheatley, who was supervising the operation, yelled to the *Dallas*'s deck crew.

"All secure?"

"All secure!" came the answer. I could feel *Nameless* applying power gradually. We churned up the water and moved forward slowly, and the cable went taut. I hoped for our sake that *Dallas* had really secured it, because a taut cable that snaps or comes loose and flies back during a towing operation is lethal. In the blink of an eye it can turn men into bloody pulp and machinery into tangled debris.

Nameless strained against the cable for what seemed like ten minutes, and the river was boiling and turning black from our props. Every once in a while we would reduce the RPMs hoping that maybe the next gradual surge would do the job. But we might as well have been trying to tow the Lincoln Memorial off its hill. And I knew the skipper was starting to worry about the strain on our engines and about the tide that was still going out. The river was getting shallower by the minute and even with our shallow draft, there was some doubt creeping in about whether we could get out of there, much less pull the *Dallas* out of the mud.

Finally, after more minutes of fruitless straining, both skippers decided it was no use.

"That'll do, Boats," yelled Ford to Wheatley from the bridge wing. "Secure from towing. We'll go alongside and pick up the Frenchman and take him back down the river."

"Aye, aye, sir," said Wheatley.

The crew on the *Dallas* let go the cable, and we pulled it in through the water and secured it. Then we turned back upstream, spinning in place by reversing one engine and going ahead with the other until we were facing *Dallas*'s stern. We moved forward and went alongside, and Rene Malevergne jumped across and landed on our quarterdeck.

"Thanks for trying, Tom," said *Dallas*'s skipper. "I think we'll be all right when the tide comes in. If not, we'll commandeer a tug. With our planes above we'll be safe from any artillery. The French seemed to be getting tired of all this, anyway."

"OK, Bob. Good luck!" We backed down until we were clear of *Dallas*'s stern and then spun around and headed down the river.

We were still at general quarters and would stay that way until we were out of the river and well out to sea. We still had twelve miles of potentially hostile river to travel.

Rene saw me at the gun and came over.

"We meet again, monsieur," he said, with a smile. "Welcome back to Morocco."

"Thank you. I wish it were under different circumstances." There was a Casablanca café and a blond chanteuse that I remembered suddenly, and fondly. Different circumstances.

"*Moi aussi*! But at least this time you are the hunter, not the duck."

I shook his hand and tried to think of some clever play on the word "*canard.*" But I couldn't come up with anything. It had been a long day, and it was still only morning.

Chapter Nineteen

The trip down the river didn't take very long. We wasted no time, and it helped that Rene was on the bridge with Captain Ford as we scooted along with the ebb tide. There were pockets of French troops scattered along both banks. I figured they were stragglers who had become separated from their units. One or two fired a shot at us, but if the bullets hit *Nameless* I didn't know about it. One or two of the more audacious Frenchmen stood up in the tall grass right along the river and gave us the bird. He could have shot any of us on deck with no trouble, but he was satisfied with a gallant Gallic gesture. We didn't shoot at him, either. Reynolds returned the bird, though, giving the American single-finger version. The Frenchman grinned and shook his fist, and I figured that the battle for the Sebou and Port Lyautey was pretty much over.

But not quite. There were still French troops holed up in the Kasbah. They were surrounded by our guys, but they were fighting back with small arms and machine guns. They didn't bother much about us as we sailed by, since they were too busy. They were about to get busier, too, because the Army called for an air strike and a half dozen Dauntless bombers showed up and pounded the French fort. We could feel the concussion from those bombs out on the river, and the smoke and flying debris were impressive. Pity the poor bastards under all that. As we passed the fort and scraped over the bar and then through the two jetties, the firing from the Kasbah fell silent.

As soon as we felt the rhythm of the Atlantic take hold of *Nameless*, the men gave a cheer and we all took a deep breath of the sea breeze. It was good to be back where we belonged.

The battle was winding down, although you wouldn't know it from looking back toward the shoreline and all up and down the beach, because there was smoke billowing everywhere and fires burning and equipment and ruined assault boats scattered here and there all along the beaches. After being bombed again, the Kasbah looked like a giant, smoking Dutch oven, *sans* lid. If Beau Geste and his brothers were still in there, they were sorry about it. Inland, there was more smoke, and there was still the desultory sound of artillery and small arms.

"Look at all that junk on the beach," said Otto. He was expressing what we all were thinking. War involves considerable waste. More of the obvious.

When we were several miles out to sea we secured from general quarters, and the captain gave the men a hearty "Well Done!" over the ship's loudspeaker. And the men gave him a cheer in response.

The sea outside the harbor and river mouth was still covered with our shipping, and now and then the big guns of the *Texas* and the *Savannah* would fire off a couple of volleys in response to a naval gunfire spotter somewhere on shore. Maybe there were French reinforcements on the road up from Rabat or coming west from Fez. There was no way to know, but if they were on the road and if a spotter saw them, they would soon be turning around and moving out of range. A well-spotted naval gun is a very dangerous weapon. If our generals learned nothing else from this invasion, they learned that.

We soon saw the *Contessa*. She was still doing her lazy circles several miles offshore. You couldn't blame her for staying in motion. With a cargo of bombs and gas she wanted to do all she could to make it as hard as possible for any U boats in the area. It was little enough, but in wartime you do all you can and then hope for the best. Still more of the obvious.

We pulled to within a couple of hundred yards of *Contessa* and put the whaleboat in the water.

Captain Ford and I went to the quarterdeck to say goodbye to Rene.

"Thank you, monsieur," said the skipper. "I hope our boys didn't mess up your town too badly."

Rene shrugged.

"We have brought it on ourselves, alas. The traitors in Vichy have caused all this. But real Frenchmen are back in the fight. This time I know our side will win." It was a good line, I thought. Maybe I'd send it to Hobey to use. Rene shook our hands. "Thank you, Captain. And you, too, Lieutenant. Perhaps we will meet again."

"I hope so, Rene. Goodbye."

"Brave fella," said the captain, as we watched the whaleboat motor over to *Contessa*.

"Yes, sir. One of the good ones."

We were ordered back on screening duty. There was still the very real danger of U boats. But we returned to a regular watch schedule.

We were steaming in our usual figure eight pattern when we came past the *Carlota*. I couldn't figure what she was doing there. She had no cargo. Maybe she was still standing by in case *Contessa* had problems and needed to transfer the bombs and gas. I suppose she had nothing else to do for the moment.

We overtook them and passed within a couple of hundred yards. Captain Flynn and Timmons were on the wing of the bridge. They recognized *Nameless* and both waved enthusiastically and gave the thumbs up as we passed their starboard side. I watched them through my binoculars, Timmons still looking like central casting for Lord Jim, Flynn for Tweedledee.

Timmons took up the handheld loud hailer.

"Don't forget our appointment in Winchester—Bass and trout and Sally Free."

I waved and gave them two thumbs up. And as we passed I heard Captain Flynn yelling something about a parrot. But I couldn't make it out.

Later that day the French general in charge down in Casablanca surrendered, and firing ceased up and down the coast of Morocco. They figured they had done enough to satisfy their sense of military honor and now were all smiles and welcoming to their new allies. In their mind, I suppose, they had not been defeated but had just decided to quit and change sides. Ironically, it was a replay in microcosm of their spat with the Germans, only with a new cast of characters. Well, as I have noticed before, when you're trying to sell yourself a story, you generally have a sucker for a customer.

About 1600 I went to my cabin and passed out on my bunk. I'd have the midwatch.

Chapter Twenty

AT 0400 THE NEXT MORNING I WENT OFF WATCH AND DOWN TO THE tiny wardroom to get something to eat. I sat down at the table. There was a window in the door between the wardroom and the galley. I could see Blake in there. Every once in a while, he would look in to see if I wanted anything, and he'd smile, hopefully.

I got some coffee and opened the letter from my Hollywood buddy, Hobey Baker.

Dear Old Sport,

I bring you hearty greetings from Neverland. People here are in surprisingly high spirits. The boys at Warners are very excited about finishing up their latest picture, called Casablanca. I think I told you, I had been asked to contribute my two cents for it, and I did. Up to the very last days of shooting there was some question about how it should end, and as usual they asked a dozen or so of us ink-stained wretches to contribute ideas. You see, it's a triangle love story, and of course those always end the same way—the strong jawed hero gives up the girl he loves for a noble cause. That's the way this one will end, too. But my ideas were different and when you see the finished product, you'll agree that mine were infinitely better, or at least fresher and maybe more realistic. I suggested that the last scene would show the hero, Rick (played by Bogie), going off with Victor Lazlo in the plane for Lisbon, leaving Ilsa (played by Ingrid Bergen) standing on the tarmac, wondering why she never suspected the two guys were "that way." But she sighs and shrugs and goes back to the café and eventually marries

Sam, the colored piano player. (Well, she's Swedish or Norwegian or something Scandinavian, so it's plausible.) Then Captain Renault and Major Strasser open a gift shop together in the bazaar, and they all live happily ever after. The last shot is a close-up of Sam with a big smile on his face. Fade out. Roll titles. I put all this in a memo to the powers that be at Warner Brothers, and the execs with a sense of humor, both of them, thought it was very funny. They're all in a good mood over there, even the ones with ulcers, because the word is there's going to be a big invasion of the real Casablanca. The one in Morocco. Somehow Jack Warner got wind of it. Not surprising since he's well connected with the people in power. The execs are wetting themselves with glee, because the movie will come out at the same time newspapers all over the world will have headlines about "Casablanca, The Battle." A dozen corrupt press agents (tautology?) couldn't come up with anything better than that! So the boys at Warners were all in such a good mood that I got another assignment to write a travelogue, this time for a place called Borneo. Ever heard of it? I hear the beaches are very nice there, so we'll be able to use a lot of stock footage from the recent Esther Williams movie, Sand in Your Skivvies. Or something like that. And if they have some Indians there, even better. We've got plenty of footage of Indians attacking wagon trains. That sort of thing may not actually happen in Borneo, but we can still use it, because who's going to know any different in Peoria? So I will be able to keep the wolf from the door for a while more at least.

The lovely and talented Hedda Gabler survived that lawsuit by the relatives of the woman who committed suicide at Hedda's suggestion. The relatives really didn't have much of a chance against the newspaper's lawyers. The lawyers proved that Hedda was being ironic, when she wrote that in her advice column. Of course, anyone with a brain would assume that. What no one knows, however, is that Hedda doesn't have an ironic bone in her head. Just the regular kind. But I make allowances, because she does have a heavenly body, as I'm sure you remember. And she has cut back on her use of chewing gum. So,

*as the old Gershwin song goes—"Who could ask for anything more?"
Not me!*

*You'll be glad to know that the starlets still swim bare-assed from
nine till midnight at the Garden of Allah pool, and the broken down,
overweight writers still stand around and wait to rescue one of them
from drowning. Or from chastity.*

*I hope you're having a fine time and staying dry. All the gang here at
the Garden send their regards, but they are sincerely glad you're not
here, because you had a way of attracting the bare-assed starlets and
putting us flabby writers in the shade, appeal-wise. And where are
you, anyway?*

Your friend from purgatory, Hobey

Hobey had no way of knowing that I was actually here and a part of the
real "Casablanca, The Battle." If he had, and if he knew what was happening, he would have used a different tone. Probably. So I had to smile.
I couldn't help noticing the nice inversion of stories—Captain Ford's
county fair where the boys go to look at the fat women, versus Hobey's
world, where the beautiful girls show up to see the fat men—one or two
of them wearing beards. It was a funhouse mirror in the Great Carnival,
I suppose. So I did have to smile, briefly.

But only briefly. I was dog tired, for one thing. For another, I couldn't
help thinking there were several hundred of our guys who'd never get
to see that new movie, having been killed in the real place. By our new
allies. And later that day, now that things had quieted down, we would
have a ceremony for Pancho and Lefty. Reynolds, our resident musician,
would play "Taps" on his trumpet. So I would leave the gleeful grins to
the boys at Warner Brothers, who would soon be basking in a million
dollars' worth of free publicity.

"Blake!" I said.

He came through the door wiping his hands on a towel.

"Yes, sir?" He was smiling, too, but very tentatively. He was hoping he might be off the shit list.

"It's been a long couple of days."

"Yes, sir. It sure has."

"How about some breakfast?"

He brightened up.

"Yes, sir. I can whip you up some bacon and eggs in no time. Or flapjacks. Or, if you'd rather, there's some franks and beans left over from the mess deck last night."

"For breakfast?"

"Oh, yes, sir. I like to have them now and then. They're good and filling when you're hungry. And they're even better the next day, after they've had a chance to sit together, you might say."

"Marinate?"

"I guess. I can get them for you in two seconds. I have some staying warm on the stove."

I looked at him and smiled.

"All right."

He grinned back at me. He really was a good soul, and harmless.

"Yes, sir. I think you'll like 'em. Coming right up." He turned to go.

"And Blake . . ."

"Yes, sir?"

"Got any fresh cornbread?"

THE END